Hi!
These books are st
What did you
like?
Not like?
Please
let me
know!
JoyBomb@pm.me

:)

HELLO GOD ?

It's me,
JOY BOMB!
FATHER KNOWS BEST

Joy Bomb Publishing

For DB
Father knew best when
He gave me you!

ISBN 978-1-7778587-1-1

Cover design by Joy Bomb
Illustrations by the AMAZING Enas_179 (Fiverr) You go girl!
Editing by Holy Spirit and trusted children's librarian, Laura Hope (she is a good secret keeper friend and an amazing editor!)

Hello God? Can I tell You Something?

Grandma moving in hasn't been a bad thing. Oh, her cooking is still vomit-trocious, but mom seems less tired and distracted . . . and less chores for me to do! SCORE!
The Fab Four has ended up being the Fab Five? Is it going to grow even more? What are You up to?
There were a LOT of whispers and secrets at school today. It felt like people were all looking at ME! Did I miss something? What is going on?

Gratitude and Thanks

Thanks that I didn't have to give grandma my room

What is God saying to me?

You are telling me to not worry about tomorrow, and to stop trying to figure everything out.
You say things are going to get bumpy? What does that even mean? Why don't You speak plainly, instead of cryptic messages? I know, I know, that is Your way. Parables and stories. Yes, I hear You. I will keep my eyes seeking YOU and not answers. What? OKAY, I am holding on!

Since You're listening . . . I kinda need . . .

You to buckle me in when the ride is getting wild!

Thank You for hearing & loving me!

Introduction

Welcome to "*Father Knows Best*"!

Joy was very brave to share a few of her journal pages with you, and we hope you will be able to keep the feelings and thoughts she shares with you a secret!

You will notice, though, that Joy did not circle or color the emoticons yet.

She thought it would be FUN if you could try and guess what she was feeling that day and circle or color it yourself. Was she feeling mostly just one emotion, or did she have a topsy-turvy day and experience several? Color as many as you choose! Feel free to look up the verses that Joy notes on her pages as well.

We hope you have one of the same journals Joy has so you too can have a place to write down your emotions, thoughts and prayers.

Enjoy meeting Joy and her friends and of course, her interactions with the spirit world!

When Joy has time, she loves to hear from her new friends. Sometimes she is too busy with chores to answer you though, so don't be discouraged if it takes her awhile to reply! JoyBomb@pm.me

Chapter 1

On this April Saturday morning, eleven-year-old Joy Bomb was enjoying the melancholy sound of rain hitting her bedroom window as she lay tucked in and cozy under her rainbow comforter. Her oldest brother, Robert, had started a new job and he left before 7am. That meant no more noisy blenders or early lectures. Joy missed seeing him around the house, but also looked forward to a slower, quieter, guilt-free sugary cereal breakfast.

Things at the Bomb house had changed drastically in the last few weeks. Joyce Neil, Helen Bomb's mother, had moved in for reals, which meant a whole bunch of adjustments. For Joy, at first there was talk about her sharing her room . . . with her grandmother! Thankfully, it was decided since Robert was rarely home during the day, he would sleep in the unfinished basement and Grandma Joyce could have his room. Joyce Neil likes to be busy and make herself useful, so she also took a lot of the chores the Bomb kids used to try to do (when they got around to them). One of the regular things she had been doing was preparing meals. However, what she created in the kitchen could barely be regarded as food. As such, all of the Bombs had learned the importance of condiments; ketchup, soy sauce, gravy, juice, vinegar . . . anything to add moisture and mask the flavor of their grandmother's concoctions. Helen appreciated the help and was sure when she stocked up on flavor-packing, side sauces to also buy jumbo, family-size bottles of antacid pills and thick, pink, stomach tonic.

Flipping over, Joy stared out the window. The seal between the two panes of glass on the bottom sliding window had broken, making the view a bit hazy, but the upper pane was clear and she could see gray misty skies. No blue was peeking through today. She smiled. Suddenly, she heard a hushed – but not hushed enough – conversation outside her door.

"Helen, that boy works too much! He's only seventeen."

Joy could hear her Grandma Joyce speaking in the hall. She was rarely without opinions and shared them freely.

Helen Bomb was busy shoving clean, rolled towels into the linen closet, ignoring her mother's comments. "I tell you, this is like me trying to put on my skinny jeans the week after Christmas! Ten pounds of potatoes in a five pound sack!"

Joy waited to see if one of them was going to come in and interrupt her bliss. She walked her fingers across the rainbow lines as she counted quietly, "One thousand . . . two thousand . . . three . . . ."

Realizing she wasn't going to be interrupted, she sighed contently and reached for the galaxy covered backpack she kept next to her bed. Her face grimaced. She had been using this same backpack for two years now. She used to like it, but now it irritated her. All of her friends got new backpacks OF THEIR CHOICE at the beginning of every school year. This backpack was not Joy's choice. It was Billy's pick and got passed down to her after he used it for barely a year.

Sure, she didn't mind when she started fourth grade to inherit Billy's cast off. In fact she always admired it and was excited and even proud of it.

But that was then.

Middle school was only a few months away, and this time, Joy was determined to start school with a little more style and fix her clumsy, accident-ridden reputation.

She unzipped the outside pocket and pulled out a small butterfly covered notebook, the one she uses to write down random thoughts, but then erases them. It was an odd quirk that Joy had discovered last year. There was something about getting things out of her head and onto paper that made her feel better, or at least help things make a bit more sense. Then, ever the practical, private person, Joy would erase every sign of whatever she had written. This too had its benefit. Joy could control something. And, she liked the smell and feel of an eraser getting hot and soft under the pressure of her hand.

Opening up to the first page – as the whole book was still blank after almost a full year – Joy began to doodle.

This backpack is ugly and I hate it!

As soon as she read what she wrote, Joy felt a crackly sound in her ears. She cleared her throat. Taking the eraser, she began to slowly watch the words disappear.

When she was finished, having done a thorough job, a pile of pink residue filled the gutter of her notebook. She ran her fingers through the mound in order to push it into the wastepaper basket on the other side of her small bed. She stopped. The soft blush colored dust engaged her senses. She rubbed it gently between her fingers. "How much eraser dust have I thrown away over the last year?" she said softly to herself.

Placing the book carefully on her bed, Joy got up and began to open and close dresser drawers. Then, her desk drawer. When an idea got into Joy's head, there was no exit for it. The only way the thought would settle down is when Joy found a solution. Her mom said Joy could be as stubborn as a tick on a dog's butt.

Grabbing her multi-colored star housecoat, Joy slid on her bright pink, fuzzy slippers and shuffled into the hall. She opened the linen closet that was sandwiched between hers and Billy's rooms. She only saw linen; towels, sheets, and tablecloths. Which made Joy chuckle as her family hadn't used a tablecloth since they moved into this house five years ago. Helen was right, it was jammed full.

Joy could hear Grandma Joyce and her mom talking in the kitchen, but being so focused on her mission, she was oblivious to their hushed tones. Walking past them, she continued her explorations, opening and closing all the kitchen cabinets and drawers. Finally, the ever amazing junk drawer yielded exactly what Joy had been looking for. Holding up an odd small black cylinder with a grey rubber lid, Joy interrupted the women's semi-private discussion, "Mom, can I have this?"

Barely looking, Helen pushed back a sweaty strand off of her forehead, "Sure Gumby." That was her mom's favorite pet name for her daughter. Her mom's face looked like she welcomed the intrusion. "Would you like me to make you some pancakes this morning?"

"Helen you-"

Before her mother could finish her sentence, Helen held up her hand to her mother and gave her a look. The kind of look that every mother and daughter knows, regardless of the age. Yet, somehow the look had switched. Grandma Joyce used to be the one who controlled the 'stop hand' signal, but now it was Helen who yielded the power.

Grandma Joyce shook her head and wandered back to her room.

Joy wasn't sure what was going on, but pancakes were a welcome treat! It wasn't even Joy's birthday! Just when she was about to accept the offer, Joy's tummy did a flip. She paused. "Oh, thanks mom, but I have been craving my maple toasties!" she lied.

Helen's smile seemed half relieved but also showed some grief. "What are your plans today, Gum?"

"Me and the gang are going over to Mrs. Solomon's house."

"The gang and I?" Helen corrected her.

"No, I don't think you would fit in with us," Joy laughed, slapping her thigh, pleased with her own humor.

Just then, the back door flew open, and Steve walked in, "I got a job!" The second of the three Bomb boys, was loud and animated.

Helen looked confused. "Steve, I thought you were still sleeping? Since when do you get up so early? Listen, I don't want you working. You barely keep up with your schoolwork as it is."

Ignoring the comment, Steve shoved his hand into the open box of maple toasties.

"Ew! Mom! Gross, Steve's hands are black!"

"They are clean," he mumbled, his mouth full of cereal, "they're just stained from all the oil changes I did." He stuck his hand back into the box, taking another helping.

"Muuuuhm, make him stop!"

Helen Bomb lightly smacked her son in the arm, "Cut it out, Steve. Get a bowl and have it with milk. We can't afford you filling up on dry cereal."

"Exactly mom," Steve said, eyes wide open, "Robert isn't the only one that can help bring in some extra money."

"Steve-"

"Mom, listen, this is not just any job. It's my dream job. Mike says I can just show up when I can and he will put me to work. I can come and go as I like! No pressure. Plus, mom, just think of it, I will be able to fix your car at the shop with all their tools and their equipment for free. You will only need to pay for parts."

Helen Bomb bit her bottom lip. It did sound promising. Mike had been her mechanic for years and was a good man.

"Okay, fine, but the minute your grades slip, I am yanking the plug on that job!"

Giving his mom a hug, Steve towered over his mom by a foot.

"When did you get so tall?" Helen said to her middle son. You're only 15! By the time you're finished high school, you'll be a giant!"

Beaming with his new employment status, Steve poked his mom in the ribs, "When did you get so skinny? You and squirt," he added, turning to his sister and sticking his finger into Joy's gut, "It's a good thing I can help keep this house stocked with maple toasties!"

Joy dropped her bowl and spoon in the sink and, grabbing the plastic vial she found in the junk drawer, turned to go finish her mission. Her tummy flipped. Rolling her eyes, she pivoted on her foot, fished the dirty dishes out of the sink and placed them in the dishwasher.

Back in her room, Joy carefully picked up the pink, dust-filled notebook.

God is so bossy!!!

Laughing, she rubbed it out, stooping to lean over and smell the melted eraser bits.

She picked up the plastic container and popped off the top. She liked the sound it made. Expecting it to be empty, Joy was surprised when she saw something metal inside.

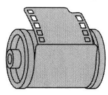

Dumping the odd find onto her bed, she picked up the notebook and, with light taps, watched the pink fluff roll into the container. She placed the lid on, dropped the metal thing-a-ma-jig into her backpack and hurried to get ready to meet her friends.

Chapter 2

"Come on Billy!" Joy waited at the top of the porch holding her and Billy's stuff as he carefully maneuvered his way up the stairs, both crutches under one arm, his other hand resting heavily on Mrs. Solomon's porch railing. Joy no longer was grossed out by the spectacle of rods sticking out of her 13-year-old brother's leg, and getting used to the sight, also meant she was losing patience with him slowing her down.

"I'm being careful; it still really hurts sometimes if it gets bumped." Billy answered her.

Three stairs might as well been Mt. Everest when trying not to bump the external fixator skeleton that still surrounded Billy's leg. It had been almost a month since he fractured it, falling out of a tree in the bog. Stuck in a wheelchair, he wasn't allowed on crutches except to do short stints across the street to visit their elderly neighbor who had been teaching them about the spirit world. Joy's friends, Jacob, Ethan and Mason who were with her when they found her brother after his fall, had become buddies with Billy during all their visits with him at the hospital. The group of four boys had been given the nickname, 'Bog-Boys'.

After telling Mrs. Solomon about the angel that caught him when he fell, Billy often joined the Fab Four girls and Mrs. S (That is what they all started to call her).

Finally up on the porch, Billy leaned against the banister, placing one crutch under each arm.

The front door was unlocked and open, so Joy pulled on the creaky screen door, holding it for Billy to hobble through.

"There they are!" Mrs. Solomon said from the other room, "Come on in Bombs!"

Making their way into the sitting room, all of Joy's earlier frustration dissipated when she saw her friends' faces. Sally, once her arch rival, now in with her besties, Sofia, her #1 since third grade, and Ava, the intense and ever spiritually curious. The girls had joined Joy and Mrs. Solomon a few weeks previous, and they had met regularly every Saturday afternoon. They also had unplanned get-togethers if anything crazy happened, but Mrs. Solomon said they would set this once-a-week time so her old screen door didn't get worn out.

Joy had a sneaky feeling it was Mrs. Solomon who was getting worn out, but for once, she didn't argue.

"Okay, now that we are all together, who would like to wash the atmosphere and welcome the Spirit of Truth?" Mrs. Solomon asked as she placed a plate of warm cookies next to the six full glasses of lemonade.

Ava, standing, raised her hands over her head. Ever since leaving the mystic club at school, she more than anyone knew the significance of what she was about to do.

With eyes wide open, she began, "Father God, we thank You that we know You hear us. As we sit together and talk about You, we know that there are spiritual beings gathering with us. You, Jesus, say that whenever two or more are gathered in Your name, You come and join us! We now speak the name and blood of Jesus over us and this room and we sanctify it –

we cleanse it – along with our own imaginations of any nefarious thoughts or spirits and only welcome You, Your angels and YOU, Holy Spirit, The Spirit of Truth to join us. In Jesus' name we pray, Amen – so be it!" Ava paused, her eyes searching the entire room.

One thing remained with Ava since she stepped out of darkness and into relationship with Jesus – Ava could still see a lot in the spirit realm. Nodding at Mrs. Solomon, they were confident the room was ready for their time together.

The rest of the group sat still, eyes closed, waiting to see if anyone would have their natural senses alerted to whatever God was trying to do in the spiritual. There was a calm, sweet presence.

"Ahhh," Mrs. Solomon released a peaceful sigh, "The Bible says we enter His presence with praise and thanksgiving! I am going to play a song. You can doodle in your books, close your eyes, sing along, or whatever your spirit moves you to do."

Mrs. S may have been old, but she had some rad speakers. Using her phone she clicked on a music app and chose a song. The boom-boom-boom of the base notes practically made the chandelier crystals move.

Sofia closed her eyes and laid her head back on the couch. Billy began to intently draw in his notebook. Ava almost immediately got off the couch and knelt on the floor, her forehead touching the rug, arms out wide from her side in a dramatic display. Sally smiling, eyes wide open, hummed to the melody with a surprisingly angelic sound.

Joy's body wanted to move. She got up and wandered to an open area by the front window and began to slowly sway, eyes closed, like a solo waltz.

When the song ended, if the atmosphere in the room had been any more peaceful, they would have all been asleep.

"Hallelujah," Mrs. Solomon said loudly, startling them. Smiling, she explained, "that means praise God!"

As Joy turned away from the window, from the corner of her eye, she saw her buddies, Jacob, Ethan and Mason riding their bikes down the road, looking back at her house laughing. They must have unsuccessfully called on Billy, not knowing he wasn't home.

Ava and Joy returned to their original spots as the Fab Five waited for their spiritual mentor to lead.

"So, can I ask if anyone wants to share what they experienced as they worshiped?"

"I wasn't worshipping," Billy said shrugging, "I felt compelled to draw something when I heard the music. It was like I saw something in my mind that completed the song."

"Wow," Sofia said softly, "That's amazing."

Joy made a bit of a sour face, "Of course he can draw too." she said quietly to herself. Ava heard and gave Joy a corrective nudge.

"Billy, I think that is worship?" Ava said, then looked at Mrs. Solomon for confirmation.

Mrs. Solomon scanned each of her apprentices' faces. "Worship is not what a lot of people think. Most think it is strictly singing songs, but that is only one form of worship. Like how Sally sang and we could all sense the intimacy in her voice. Moving and letting your body express what is in your heart – like Ava did by humbling herself, or Joy did by a solitary dance with her love, Jesus, is another form of worship. Sofia, I believe you were just finding peace and rest in God. And . . . Billy . . . Ava is correct. What you drew was putting the music into a picture! All of you were worshipping God in a unique way as The Spirit of Truth led you."

The five nodded, put their heads down, and scribbled what they had just learned in their notebooks.

"So," Mrs. Solomon continued, "Who wants to share first?"

No longer was it just Joy who showed up, showering her neighbor with questions. Now each one would bring their questions or share what they had learned from God themselves, and their mentor would listen, checking her ancient black book.

Billy leaned forward to try and adjust the pillow Joy had placed under his leg when she propped it up on Mrs. Solomon's coffee table. He winced, and Sofia quickly came to help.

Joy rolled her eyes.

"Well, I have a question," Sally asked, leaning in to eat a cookie while it was still warm.

The older lady nodded at Sally, indicating for her to share.

"What's a denomination? When I told someone about us coming together to learn, they used that word."

"Hmmm, well, at one time, God's family was one big united body of people. But then over time, disagreements broke out. People left one group to meet together separately. They would set up their own understanding of what God said or wanted. Then, after a while, the two groups would grow and - with more people – came more opinions and interpretations of what the Bible said. So they would divide again. And again. And again. Each time, they would create a new name for their group which we call denominations. Sometimes, it was as simple as one group liked to worship quietly, while another liked drums and guitars."

"Steve would choose that denominator," Joy said laughing. When her brother wasn't under a hood, he was practicing his guitar with his band in his friend's garage. Maybe he just really liked the smell of oily rags and gasoline.

"That sounds like our family," Billy said quietly.

No one moved. Divorce was normal in most big towns and cities, but in their small town, Helen Bomb's situation had been on full display to all. Seven years later, it was still a topic of gossip and speculation.

"Okay, well, Billy is right. Disagreements happen almost everywhere people are involved. Even families. And Joy, the word is denomination, not denominator."

"Well, a denominator is part of a fraction. And it sounds like God's family fractures a lot. Like Billy's leg."

Sofia reached for her lemonade, "I sure hope it doesn't happen to our group!" she looked intently at Billy.

The room grew solemn.

"I think we need to take a moment and build up the Spirit in this room. The Spirit of Truth gets very sad whenever He hears about the family of God being divided. Shall we play another song?"

The five nodded energetically. Mrs. Solomon picked up her cell and scrolled through her favorite playlist. Billy flipped over the page in his notebook, sharpening his pencil as he waited, and the girls all giggled.

Joy, remembering the metal thing-a-ma-jig in her backpack, bent over and fished it out. She held it up quietly, shrugging her shoulders and giving her friends a quizzical look. Ava and Sally shrugged their shoulders back at her, but Sofia's eyes lit up with excitement.

Whispering, she leaned towards Joy, "I know what that is. It's full of pictures! It's from the olden days. We use sim cards now to store photos. Lucky for you, my mom does something in our basement with those!"

Joy dropped the metal thing-a-ma-jig into Sofia's open hand and all four girls smiled. A mystery!

Hello God? Can I tell You something...

I am sorry that Your family got fractured. And keeps fracturing.
I'm sad to even think about it.

I am trying to be patient with Billy and I know You are happy he is learning about You and stuff, but why did You give him so much talent and me so little? Will I ever be as good as him?
Why does Billy keep talking about our family being broken? I think it's pretty good?

What kind of pictures are on that thing-a-ma-jig? Did You plan for me to find that tubey thing?
I gotta go soon. The girls are coming for a sleepover!

Today I feel

Gratitude and Thanks

*Thanks for not putting Your whole family in a timeout

*Thanks that Sofia knew what the black metal thing was! A mystery awaits us! Who knew pictures aren't only stored in phones?

You cry?
Oh.
Wow.
I didn't know that You got sad too.

What is God saying to me about this?

What? Oh, every good Father gets sad when His kids fight?

That is deep. Like, drowning Grandma Joyce's dry meatloaf with gravy deep. Pardon ME? Oh. So she cooks things to death (even though they are already dead) because she doesn't want any of us to get sick? Does she know how backwards that is?

I am glad that You forgive us for fighting and now that I know it makes You cry, I will try to be nicer to Billy. I'm still amazed I can call You DAD. I love that so much.

Since You're listening,
I kinda need . . .

*A New PRETTY
backpack
*To help Billy see You
as Dad too. He won't
talk about it.
*For Sofia's mom to
give us the photos
ASAP!

Thank You for hearing &
loving me!

21

Chapter 3

Legs and arms were flung all over Joy's bedroom floor. Pillows of various colors and sizes covered groggy heads. Sleepovers didn't occur very often at the Bomb house, but when they did, they were MEMORABLE!

Still half-asleep, the girls laid on top of each other in order to fit in the small space. Last night, Joy and Sally had pushed Joy's bed into the corner to make more room, and the four of them managed to squish together.

After the crazy part of the night was over, they laid in the dark with their heads together, and whispered in hushed tones. They talked about EVERYTHING! The kinds of things most wouldn't want to talk about with the lights on. Secret stuff. Joy was so happy to have girls around instead of just brothers. Sofia's dad was a doctor, so she explained a lot about how their bodies were changing and stuff. Ava shared about some of the things they used to do in the mystic club - it made the room feel creepy though so they quickly turned the lights back on and painted their nails. The girls discussed makeup and which boys they thought were cute, funny or smart. They had giggled and whispered into the wee hours of the morning, until Grandma Joyce finally came and told them to turn out the lights and go to sleep.

The sun had been up for hours but the girls were not. Sofia rolled over onto a half-eaten bag of ketchup flavored chips. A Fab Four favorite.

* * *

CRACKLE

Ava started to giggle.

Then Joy started.

Next, Sally snorted, which made Sofia laugh so hard, she started to squeal for fear of peeing her pants.

"I gotta goooooooo!" Sofia stumbled on pins and needles legs that had been wedged under someone, cutting off the circulation.

As soon as Sofia left the room, Sally flipped over and put her face up close to Joy's, "What is the deal with Sofia and Billy? Does she like him?"

"Ugh, Sofia likes everyone! Last month she had a crush on Jacob." Ava said, shoving her hand into the crushed chips.

Joy and Sally's hands joined Ava's in the bag.

Suddenly, Joy put her finger up to her lips, signaling the girls to be quiet. She pointed to Billy's room that was across the hall. He was laughing.

"Can he hear us?" Ava whispered.

Sally stood slowly, her finger over her mouth now too, gesturing to Sofia as she walked back in the room. Her eyes darted, taking in the messy surroundings. Suddenly, she got more focused. She bent down low and reached under the desk by the door. With a tug, she pulled off some silver ductape. A small microphone was stuck underneath it. Eyes grew wide. Sitting on the floor, she pulled off some more tape, slowly releasing a thin clear wire that was effectively hidden behind the leg of the desk. It ran along the baseboard and under the nearby door. Sally, now on all fours crawled and opened the bedroom door. The other 3 also hit their knees and followed closely behind.

Maybe it was all the junk food, or maybe it was the intensity of the moment, but one of them tooted. Having been crawling along in a nose-to-butt train, the offensive stench caused the girls to buckle and fall onto their sides, gagging.

"That's gross!"

"Ewwww!"

"That's what you call a failed 'clande-scent' mission." Sally groaned, laying in front of the linen closet. Joy was close behind, curled up in a ball, plugging her nose. Sofia and Ava lay in a heap in Joy's bedroom doorway. As they moaned, still covering their noses, Billy's door flew open. He wheeled past them so fast, there was nothing they could do.

Crawling on her belly like a soldier, Sally crept into Billy's room, still following the wire. On the end, there was only a plug. Billy had either listened to their conversations through his phone, a speaker . . . or . . . worse yet . . . had the microphone plugged into an mp3 recording device.

"Oh, the conversations we had last night!" Ava said, eyes looking wild.

Sofia's face went beat red.

Sally, not one to be embarrassed about anything, was too busy being impressed with Billy's brains and his execution of the plan.

"Muuuuuuuum!" Joy screamed so loud, the whole Bomb house could hear. Quickly followed by, "Billy, prepare to DIE!"

Their fun-filled night now needed some damage control.

Hello God? Can I tell You something...

I thought You were going to watch over me and have my back?!
Billy played innocent. He kept laughing the way he does. Mom must have known we were telling the truth, yet she kept telling ME to settle down?

Where is the justice?

Did Billy record our conversations?

Books I am reading or Bible Verses

I'm too upset to read anything!

What all did he hear? God, are You listening? Why did You give me stupid brothers and no sisters? And, while we are at it, let's just talk about something. I know I'm adopted. Everyone in my family has brown hair. Everyone but me! Is that what the stares and whispers at school are all about? Not just at school, but now Grandma and mom keep having weird secret talks. Couldn't You have placed me in a family with not so many boys?

Today I feel

Gratitude and Thanks

- Zip
- Nada
- Nope
- Just poop

I'm so mad, I don't want to listen tonight.

Goodnight!

What is God saying to me about this?

Since You're listening, I kinda need . . .

Witness protection

Thank You for hearing & loving me!

Chapter 4

Joy arrived at school a few minutes early, hoping to have a chance to talk with the gang. Sally was already there, waiting out in front of the entrance doors, motioning Joy to hurry and join her.

Impatient, Sally ran down the sidewalk to close the gap between them quicker. "Joy! I was thinking about something!"

"What's that? How my life is over because Billy knows absolutely everything about me now?"

"No . . . well . . . yes." Sally's face was serious. "Joy, I was thinking, Billy told your mom he had been with us all afternoon, and that he didn't do it. That he COULDN'T do it."

"Sally, get a grip! The wire went into his room and mom never even came to look." Joy shook her head and did her best Helen Bomb impression, "You just settle down, Joy Amelia Bomb, I will not tolerate you yelling in my house-"

Butting in, Sally cut Joy's rambling off and grabbed Joy's shoulders so she would look her in the eyes. "Joy. Think about it. Billy is barely mobile. Your mom was right. There was no way he could have crawled under the desk and placed that mic!"

Joy's forehead wrinkled. "But then how did it get there?"

"Joy. He had to have an accomplice."

The two girls stood silently, both of them with one hand holding their chins as they pondered possibilities.

Joy's eyes grew wildly large. "No. No. No. NO!"

"What? Do you know who helped him? Was it one of your other brothers?"

"No. Steve and Robert were both at work all day."

"Then who?"

Joy's chin dropped, her shoulders slumped. "Kill me. Kill me now and put me out of my misery. It was. It was. The Bog Boys."

Joy explained to Sally how she had seen Jacob, Mason and Ethan riding their bikes away from her house when they were at Mrs. Solomon's.

"But how did they get in?" Sally asked.

"Oh, knowing my genius brother, he probably told them when we were meeting and unlatched his window. They just crawled in after we left."

"This was premeditated then. Preplanned crimes are more serious and get longer jail time," Sally said thoughtfully. Having parents who were lawyers, she was always adding interesting tidbits about the justice system. "Do you think they all listened to the recording yet?" Sally asked, her face looking pained.

Joy and Sally's eyes met. They had to let the other two girls know what they figured out before they got to class.

The four girls went to their desks, keeping their eyes low. It was decided that Sally – being the best sleuth amongst them – would determine whether or not the fifth grade Bog-Boys had heard their 'not-so-private' conversation. Not only was she the most sneaky, she also had said the least during the night. Joy figured it was because Sally knew the importance and wisdom of 'you have the right to remain silent'.

Sitting at her desk, Joy began to write in her book.

I will never, ever talk with ANYONE ever about ANYTHING!!

She took her eraser and angrily rubbed out the words. Normally, this made her feel better, but not this time. She would try again.

I am so stupid and I talk too much!!

So full of rage, as she energetically scrubbed the words, she accidently ripped the page. "Great." She muttered. Remembering the grey plastic cylinder, Joy reached into the outside pocket of her oh-so-ugly backpack and fetched it. She pushed all the pink dust into a pile on the desk, swept them into the canister, and returned it to its pouch. A flush began to roll down Joy's face. Her cheeks were getting rosy. Thankful her hair was down, she leaned forward, trying to cloak herself. Red ears poked through her long tresses. "Psssssst," Jacob was whispering across the aisle.

Joy continued to stare at her notebook.

"Pssssssssst!"

Joy ignored him.

"Pssssssssssst!"

"Jacob," Ms. Sinclair said from the front of the class, "Is there something important that you wish to share with the whole class?"

All four girls sat like statues in their desks.

"Um, no Ms. Sinclair. I was just trying to tell Joy that she dropped something."

All eyes in the room turned in unison to look at Joy. She turned, horrified, finally looking at Jacob. He pointed to the ground under her chair where the camera film container lay at her feet.

Ms. Sinclair walked over to Joy's desk, her hand out in front of her, "What do you have there, Miss. Bomb?"

Reaching down, Joy picked up her precious pink dust collection and dropped it into her teacher's hand.

Popping off the lid, Ms. Sinclair looked into the container, and stuck her finger in. Taking a pinch, she smiled at Joy and handed it back with the lid. She leaned over, whispering in Joy's ear, "I love the smell and texture too!"

Then, with a stern look, she said loudly, "Joy, please put that away," and turning on the heel of her practical but pretty shoes, she went back to the whiteboard and continued to explain how to divide fractions.

Chapter 5

Joy practically stomped all the way home, but instead of turning north into her own driveway, she walked south across the road where she found Mrs. Solomon pulling weeds from her front lawn.

"Well, hello Joy!" Mrs. Solomon's smile disappeared, however, when she saw her young friend's face. "Well, that face is not full of peace." The elderly neighbor rose from the padded kneeling tray, flipped it upside down where it magically became a bench. She took a seat. "What is going on?"

"Mrs. Solomon," Joy said, her arms crossed tightly, "I want Billy kicked out of our group!"

The neighbor's eyebrows rose high on her forehead, "Well, whatever for!"

"Because, he is a nasty stinkweed!" Joy declared.

"Do you want to elaborate on that a bit?"

Joy stood, arms still crossed, tapping her foot. As she did, Jacob, waved at her as he pushed Billy towards the makeshift ramp of their home. Mason and Ethan followed behind.

Suddenly, Joy heard the muffled sound of her lame bright fuchsia cell phone. She quickly dug it out of her bag. "Sorry, I better answer."

Mrs. Solomon nodded.

"Joy? It's me, Sally. Okay, I chatted with Mason and I can tell you – he hasn't heard anything yet from Billy's recording. I don't think any of them have. When I stopped to ask Mason a question about tomorrow's assignment, all three of them looked and talked normal. But listen, they said they had to go push Billy home from the middle school. You better stop them from going into your house when they get there."

Joy had been wandering in the yard as Sally spoke, but now quickly turned to face her house. The boys were no longer in the front yard.

"Mrs. Solomon! I gotta go!"

Joy ran into her home, and, leaving her shoes on, flew down the hall towards Billy's room.

"Joy Bomb," her Grandma Joyce yelled, "just what do you think you are doing wearing your shoes in the house?"

Ignoring her grandmother, Joy flung open Billy's closed bedroom door. Billy was not there. No one was.

"Grandma, where is Billy?" Joy yelled as she began to snoop around the empty room.

"Oh, so now you will acknowledge me?" Grandma Joyce said, standing in the doorway. "Do you want to tell me what's going on? Should you be in here invading your brother's privacy?"

Joy spun on her heel and looked at her grandmother, "Billy's privacy? Are you kidding me right now?"

With a stomp, she slid past Joyce Neil and took off out of the house.

It only took forty large steps to reach Mrs. Solomon's yard from the Bomb's front door. Joy had been counting to herself for years. She liked to count randomly. It helped her to feel a bit more control in what Joy felt was an out of control world.

Seeing her young friend trudging towards her house, Gwen Solomon pushed herself up off the ground using the rails on her handy kneeling bench. Then, once again, she flipped it upside down, sat, and waited.

"Oh, Mrs. Solomon, I am so mad. I am going to KILL Billy!"

Not saying a word, the older neighbor reached down, picked up a thermos, and took a swig.

"Oh, let me guess. You think I am a drama queen. That's what my mom said. Are you under Billy's charming spell too?"

The old lady closed her eyes and took a deep breath. She placed her hand on her belly.

Joy knew she was interfacing with God. It was what Mrs. Solomon called praying. As mad as Joy was at Billy and God, she knew enough to be quiet.

Finally, Gwen opened her eyes and looked at Joy. Without saying a word, she turned her bench back upside down, took a trowel and began to dig up dandelion weeds again. "Joy, would you please hand me that tool?" the neighbor asked kindly, pointing to a long metal rod.

Surprised, Joy robotically complied.

"Come here and see something," she tapped the ground with the long handled tool.

For a moment, Joy's curiosity overtook her anger. She knelt down on the cool, thick deep grass next to Mrs. Solomon.

"Watch this. This thing is a game changer!" Placing the tool at the base of a large spreading dandelion, the old lady gave the long handle a push and out the weed popped.

"Oh gosh darn it!" she exclaimed, looking at the root.

"What?" Joy said, fascinated and almost thankful for the diversion from her emotional pain. "You got it out. It worked."

"Well, you would think I did," she said, clucking her tongue in displeasure, "but look, see here?" she pointed to the blunt broken end on the root. I didn't get the whole root! The tail and the tendrils are still in the ground, which means it still has life in it and will keep growing."

The old lady shook her head in disgust and, still holding the weed, raised herself up, flipped the bench and took a seat.

"Weeds, Joy Bomb, are like buried unhealthy emotions. The longer they grow, the deeper and more stubborn the roots get." She passed Joy the limp dandelion. "Often, we can allow anger, bitterness or unforgiveness to grow in our bellies – that is just one place of many where we feel and store our emotions – and before we know it, ugly, unprocessed emotions make a mess, and interfere with us experiencing other good feelings that God created for us to enjoy." Gwen's eyes perused the grass around her. She got up, took the tool and bent over. With a push and a wiggle, she easily pulled up a tiny weed.

She dropped it into Joy's hand.

"You see," Mrs. Solomon pointed to the tender root. "I got it all this time. Because the weed hadn't had time to grow stubborn and stronger than me!" she paused, tilting her head to look at Joy.

Joy brought her hand up over her heart. Then slowly it dropped to her belly. "What is growing in me?"

"Well, why not take a few moments and ask God?"

Joy closed her eyes.

Mrs. Solomon pulled off her garden gloves and rubbed her fingers. She wasn't as young as she used to be.

Opening her eyes, Joy looked at her neighbor. "I'm stubborn, and impatient, but I think the biggest weed is . . . anger."
Nodding, Gwen Solomon stood, opened her arms wide and the young girl leaned into her. It took exactly five counts and one hard hug before Joy broke and months if not years of tears flowed.
Mrs. Solomon held her tighter. "Joy, now that you've worked that buried emotion a bit, wiggling and loosening some of those bitter roots with your tears, I think it would also help if you had a listening ear. Give your mom a call to tell her you're here, and then come inside and we can talk."
Wiping her nose on the back of her hand, Joy sniffled, "Mom is not home, but I will call Grandma. I need to apologize to her anyhow."

The lemonade wasn't fresh but was still refreshing.

Joy slouched back into the couch, "So you can see, Mrs. Solomon, what a stinkweed Billy was." She took a sip of her lemonade having told her neighbor all about the devastating sleepover privacy invasion.
"Well, what Billy did was completely unkind and unacceptable. And he didn't just hurt you, he invaded all the girls' privacy."

Sitting straight up, Joy felt better already. Finally, an adult validated her. "So we can kick him out of the group?"

"Joy, is that what God would want us to do?"

Joy's left foot sat on top of her right, her toes wrapping around each other like a monkey. Billy liked to call her monkey toes. Taking a deep breath, Joy looked at her older friend. "No, I think the only way God can get the stink out of Billy's weed is for Billy to learn more about sin and God's love and stuff."

The old lady laughed, and as she stood, let out an "oomph!" as she rubbed her back. "Oh, I think my back is not what it used to be. Maybe I'm too old to be living here on my own with all this yardwork."

"Mrs. Solomon, you can't move. My life would end. I would die without you!" Joy jumped up and wrapped her long thin arms around her old neighbor's neck, clinging tightly. "Promise me you'll never move!"

Chapter 6

When Joy walked into her house, she was greeted by the most offensive smell ever. Pausing at the front door, she pulled out her little notebook and hastily wrote.

What on earth is this stench?
Maybe I will feed my plate to Billy

That made her laugh, and it felt good to feel joyful instead of angry. Pulling out her eraser, she rubbed out the words, being careful to keep the soft dust in the gutter of the book. She gently tucked the notebook into her back pocket. Her dust transfer to the cylinder container would have to wait!

Walking into the kitchen, Joy saw Grandma Joyce, all sweaty and covered in flour.

"What's for dinner, Grandma?" Joy asked, trying to hide the fear in her voice.

"Pork chops!" Grandma Joyce answered. "They've been in the oven for a while now. Did you want to help me check them while you tell me what on earth had you behave so rudely to me today?"

Joy pulled an apron off a hook on the wall, tying it behind her back. "How long have they been in the oven, Grandma?"

Grandma tucked a piece of loose hair behind her ear. "Gumby," Joy's grandma had begun to call Joy by the nickname her mom gave her. Joy wasn't too sure how she felt about that. "Can you please pass me that thermometer?" Oven mitted hands pointed to a device that looked like a clock.

"Grandma?" Joy said again as she waited next to her grandmother. Steam, or maybe smoke rose from the dry meat. "How long was THAT in the oven?"

"What time is it dear?"

Joy looked at the clock stuck in the meat. It wasn't a clock. She looked up at the wall, "It's 5:30 now."

"Baby girl, can you read the dial on this contraption?" Joyce Neil was inches away from the hot casserole dish, waving her hand in an attempt to disperse the smoke.

"Um, it's all the way to the right . . . 200?"

"Perfect!" Grandma Joyce clapped her still mitted hands.

Joy looked at the shrunken pieces of meat. Were they still considered meat? Or were they charcoal? "Grandma, what time did you put the pork chops in the oven?"

"Oh, after lunch sometime," she answered.

Joy covered her face with her hands. This was going to be the worst dinner ever. She began to look through the cupboards, opening and closing doors in search of the best gravy substitute.

"Now, Joy, what was going on with you today?" Grandma Joyce said, smiling with satisfaction at her 'well-cooked' meal.

She plugged in the kettle and dumped a bag of dehydrated potatoes into a metal bowl to make a side dish, dropping a blob of soft butter on top of the dry flakes.

Joy sat down on a stool by the island and, just as she was about to start to babble, remembered what Ms. Sinclair had told her once, "Sometimes it's better to give people a short version instead of going on and on and on."

"Billy and the other three Bog-Brats stuck a microphone in my room the night of our sleepover."

"So it was true?" Grandma said, surprised.

"Yes! If Mom had just listened . . ." Joy caught herself before she gave waaaaay too many details.

"Well, what shall we do, Miss Joy?" Grandma asked as she stirred madly. Slop in the metal bowl splattered all over the counter.

Suddenly, Joy had an idea!

Joy leaned up against her front window, a smile crossing her face. There, across the street in Mrs. Solomon's yard were the Bog-Boys. Billy in his wheelchair, with various tools on his lap 'supervising' as Mason, Jacob and Ethan were spread out all over the yard, pulling weeds, raking last fall's leaves, and even planting a few spring flowers!

Billy told his grandmother that he only listened for a few minutes during the night, but then pulled the plug when they starting talking about personal stuff. Then, the next morning, he tried again, but the girls found the microphone. There was nothing recorded, so the other boys never heard anything. Billy promised he never even told them what he had heard.

Joy believed him. So did Grandma. But, Grandma Joyce told him there are penalties when we sin, and justice would be served. Their collective punishment was fair, just and swift!

Joy pulled out the small notebook and pencil from her back pocket.

who knew that something as bad as the Bog-Boy invasion could end up so good?

Hello God? Can I tell You something...

I'm sorry. I guess I was just a big stinkweed to You, like Billy was to me. You have to live in me, and I let anger and bitterness crowd You. Did You get squished?

Once I was on the airport train and people just get coming in and in and in until I was pressed up hard against the back.

Was that how You felt in me? Is that why I haven't felt You moving in my tummy lately?

Anyhow, I know You already forgave me cuz it all worked out. Maybe instead of weeding, they should have all had to eat grandma's pork chops. Even she said they were inedible!

Oh, one last question . . . why are grandma and mom so whispery all the time lately?

Today I feel

Gratitude and Thanks

*Thanks for justice

*Thanks that mom ordered a pizza tonight!

You are telling me that I should be learning to trust You more. That I have seen You get me out of a few pickles already in my eleven years on this planet.

what is God saying to me about this?

That's good and true.
what?

Oh, sometimes parents are quiet and wait for their kids to figure things out. You never left me – even though I couldn't feel You moving as much.

whew. Oh, and You don't get squished, but You don't appreciate sharing Your space with stinky, smelly attitudes.
Yikes! Okay!

Since You're listening, I kinda need . . .

Grandma to SERIOUSLY get some cooking lessons!

Thank You for hearing & loving me!

Chapter 7

Jacob, Mason and Ethan gave the girls the cold shoulder at school the next day. Nobody likes to have their friends snitch on them, even if what they did was wrong.

Joy sat in class, having given up on connecting with her Bog-Boy friends who refused to look at her. Her eyes drifted from desk to desk, examining each face. Last week she thought it was her crazy imagination running wild, but today she knew something was up. Most of her classmates would not return Joy's stare, but quickly looked away.

Joy took out her small notepad.

I am not crazy.
It's like there is
something going on,
but I am the last to
know!

She rubbed it out and tried again.

Maybe I am adopted
and my birth parents
are rich and famous!
Or maybe I am a long
lost princess!

Snickering at the outrageous things she had just written, Joy rubbed out her thoughts, being careful to make a neat pile of pink eraser dust in the corner of her desk to deposit into her plastic canister at their next break time, as per Ms. Sinclair's suggestion.

When the lunch bell rang, Joy gave the other Fab Four girls their special, subtle hand gesture that Sally had made up. A signal to meet at the rope ladder for their rooftop rendezvous.

Sally, back in the day when she was the school's misunderstood bully, had ingeniously installed a rope ladder up on the small basketball storage shed. They used a hidden branch to pull it down whenever they needed a private place to meet at lunch. It used to be just Sally's secret place, but now it was all of theirs.

Once they were all up and seated under the willow tree's cloaking branch, Joy cleared her throat, "Okay, so I get the feeling that I am the last to know something. Why is everyone acting so weird around me?"

Sally looked down and began to flick dry leaves off a few loose roofing tiles.

Ava did what she always did when she was nervous, she started to peel off her nail polish.

Joy turned to Sofia, who was frozen. Her eyes were large.

"Sofia, you better tell me what I don't know."

The other two girls looked at Sofia and shook their heads.

"Well, we know you don't like talking about it, Joy, so we just don't."

"What are you talking about?" Joy was getting exasperated.

"You know," Ava said even quieter than their normal rooftop meeting talk, "It's about your dad."

Joy smacked her hand hard against the tile roof beneath her. An imprint of the pebbly surface stung. "Oh my goodness, that was like forever ago! Why are people all blah blah blah about that again?" Joy made talking puppet gestures with her hands.

The three girls looked at each other.

Sofia spoke first, "Well, my family never even lived here back when he . . um . . . ."

"Just drop it," Joy cut her friend off, "I really don't want to talk about this!"

Sofia decided to break the tension with some good news, "Hey, my mom is going to do the thing she does with your thing-a-ma-jig tonight. She said if she sees one more tax return she will scream, so she needs a break."

"So, you can bring them to school tomorrow?" Joy asked.

Sofia raised her hands up in the air a bit as if to catch something, "Maybe. It takes a while for them to dry out."

"Dry out?" Ava and Sally said in unison.

"Ya, she soaks them in stuff and they are all wet, then she hangs them on a string. Like laundry."

The girls giggled at the thought of soaking photos and hanging them on a string.

"I hope she doesn't hang them next to your dad's underwear!" Joy said, laughing a bit.

"No silly, she has a special room where she does it. It has to be dark in there."

"I wonder whose pictures they are." Sally asked, thankful the conversation had changed directions as her dad had explained to her about lawyer-client privilege. Sally wasn't allowed to tell Joy anything she had accidently heard her parents discussing.

"Well, I guess my mom's?" Joy said, shrugging. The angry red glow was slowly disappearing as she took a few deep breaths. Ava leaned in, motioning to the others to come closer in their circle, "Maybe we should pray before we go back to class," she looked at Joy. "I know you are feeling stuff and maybe God can help you feel better?"

Joy smiled at her friend. "Sure. Maybe a quick one?"

The four girls closed their eyes, and quieted their minds so they could give God their full attention.

"Father God," Ava began quietly, "Thanks for promising to be with us, even when things are weird. My friend Joy is getting plucked to death like a chicken these days with so many

unfair things. Thanks for catching the boys in their prank and making it good for us, and for Mrs. Solomon. Please be with us and especially Joy today. We thank You that you're a good Dad to all of us, in Jesus name, Amen, so be it."

"Amen, so be it," the other three said quietly, giggling a bit from the chicken comment.

Gwen Solomon had told them that God had a sense of humor, so the girls were trying more and more to make Him laugh. They figure He has to put up with an awful lot of boring prayers, so they might as well lighten things up for their Heavenly Father.

The four girls placed their hands over each other's the way the soccer players did before a match. They all looked at Joy, waiting for her to start their closing group chant.

"God Rules!" Joy whispered, and as she did, she lifted her hand, fluttering her fingers towards the sky.

"God reigns!" Sofia said softly, doing the same with her hand.

"God's won!" Sally said, fluttering her hand up.

Ava's hand hung suspended solo, with a dramatic pause, she looked Joy in the eye, "It's DONE!" her fingers flying up just like the others.

Chapter 8

The firemen were just leaving as Joy walked up to her house. Billy and the other Bog-Boys were out front.

"What is going on?" Joy asked.

The four boys turned to her, looked at each other, and then back at Joy.

"Well guys, shall we break our vow of silence against her?" Mason asked, giving Joy a crooked grin.

"Oh, I guess so, seeing as our house almost burnt down to the ground," Billy said.

"Our house?" Joy dropped her backpack onto the sidewalk in shock.

Joy and Billy looked at each other.

"Grandma," they both said at the same time, although Billy's voice was telling and Joy's tone was questioning.

"Yup," Billy said, "She really did it this time."

"Is Grandma okay?" Joy asked, her voice quivering a bit.

"Oh yeah, she's okay," Mason said, rubbing Joy's shoulder. "The firemen said she is totally fine. The oven, on the other hand, is not."

"Whew," Joy bent over to pick up her backpack. As she did, a car drove by, slowing down in front of Mrs. Solomon's house. There was a picture that covered the whole vehicle, one of those advertising kinds, "Call Ralph for all your realty needs! 555-SOLD" Joy read out loud. "What are realty needs?" she asked to whomever would answer.

"That's my uncle. He sells houses," Ethan answered. "He's from the city though. I wonder why he's out here?"

Joy's heart began to beat so fast, she thought she was going to drop to the ground. Only this time instead of a dodgeball hitting her in the head like the last time she almost passed out, it was something harder - the thought of losing one of her best friends.

As they talked, Helen Bomb's car turned into the driveway. Joy shook her head, waved goodbye to her friends and rushed towards the rear garage to meet her mom.

"See you later, Joy!" Mason called.

Jacob wheeled Billy up the ramp, "Thanks, Jacob," Billy said, dismissing his help, "I can manage from here by myself."

Helen and Joy entered the house from the back door, as Billy wheeled himself towards the kitchen through the front hall. There, at the table sat Joyce Neil, looking as over done as the smoking chicken carcass on the counter.

"What happened?" Helen asked her mother, her eyes on the soot covered cupboard next to the stove.

"Oh, the silly bird. They must have sold me an expired one. It was all dried out so it cooked too fast . . . it . . . caught on fire."

Helen Bomb stared at her mother, and then the smoking bird. Joy kept her eyes on her own mother, and wondered if steam or smoke was going to come out of her ears. There was going to be a 'mother-daughter' conversation, and Joy didn't want to be a witness. In case there was a crime committed. Sally had taught her that.

"Mom, I gotta run over to see Mrs. S. I won't be long!" she finished the sentence as she ran out the back door.

"Your homework?" Mrs. Bomb yelled without getting a response from her daughter. Turning to Billy, as Grandma began to pick at the incinerated fowl, she mouthed to her son, "Chinese or pizza?"

Joy looked both ways before she ran across the street, and it was a good thing she did, as the realtor and family were getting out of the car on the side street a block down from their house. In his hand, Ethan's Uncle Ralph held up a set of keys, and extended them towards the man and woman with him. The man had a baby in his arms.

She didn't even bother counting her steps, but ran as fast as she could up the porch steps, and banged on the front screen door as she rang the doorbell. Gwen Solomon came to the door.

"Joy Bomb, my word, where's the fire?"

Joy pushed her way into the foyer and closed the door, "Well, it was at our house, but it's out now! Mrs. Solomon, are you moving?" Joy asked nervously, her back to the door. She covered the doorway with her body, trying to block anyone from entering.

"Oh my goodness, Joy, I just said that the other day because I was aching from weeding. Someday I may have to sell my home, but not yet . . . Lord willing," she added under her breath.

"Whew," Joy turned and peeked out the side window. The family was nowhere to be seen.

"Well, I don't have time to talk today, Joy. Is that all you came for? And, I wasn't going to ask, but I assume the sirens I heard then had something to do with your Grandmother?"

The two looked at each other and laughed, "Yep!" Joy nodded. "And I think mom is burning mad!"

Hello God? Can I tell You something...

I am not having the best days. I thought once You and I became good friends, my life would be . . . perfect.

But it's not.

You do help me – A LOT – but there are still so many problems that keep popping up. Problems popping up like weeds is what Mrs. S would say.

Can I ask You something? Why are people so mean and gossipy? Why do they keep talking about what my dad did when that was like . . . forever ago? I was in preschool and now I am in fifth grade. Why can't You erase the past?

Today I feel

Gratitude and Thanks

*Thanks for saving our house from fire

*Thanks that Mrs. S isn't moving!

Just because You are my Father, doesn't mean You stop the world from spinning?

What is God saying to me about this?

Can You help a girl out? What does that mean? Oh. You don't spin the world backwards and undo history . . . not even for me. But You can help us manage the damage.

Well, that's good. I guess. If You WERE ever going to spin the world backwards and redo history, can You not just fix the mess with my missing in action dad, but could You also send Grandma Joyce to cooking school?

(Did I make You laugh with that one?)

Since You're listening, I kinda need . . .

Sofia's mom to finish the picture thingy that she's doing.

Thank You for hearing & loving me!

Chapter 9

The mirror reflected a plain, boring face. Joy pushed her nose back and forth with critical eyes. Moving on from there, she moved closer to the mirror and traced her pale, barely there eyebrows. She licked her finger and ran the spit across the brows and like magic, they were a teeny bit more noticeable. Encouraged, she opened the medicine cabinet and began to search.

What she was searching for, she wasn't sure. Not makeup. Not in this house. Helen Bomb had naturally dark eyelashes and brows that matched her thick, almost black hair . . . just like the rest of her brothers. Yet another reason that caused Joy to often lay awake at night and wonder if she was truly a blood Bomb.

Disgusted, she closed the medicine cabinet and stared at her now dry, fair eyebrows. What could she do to keep them wet, or to tint them?

"Coffee," Joy said quietly.

She looked at the time on her phone and figured she had a few minutes to experiment before school. She slid down the wooden hall in her slippers, stopping in expert style right at the entrance to the kitchen. Her mother and grandma had taken out the contents of the scorched cupboard the night before. Joy's hand hunted amongst the various size bottles of sauces and tins of spices. There, near the back, was a small bottle of dry instant coffee that Helen kept for 'emergencies' when she would run out of the 'good stuff'.

Joy tucked the small jar into her housecoat and ran back to the bathroom.

"Where are you off to in such a hurry?" Grandma Joyce asked when Joy almost knocked her over.

"Bathroom!" she answered.

Joy almost smashed her face as she was going so fast and didn't expect to find a closed door. Someone had taken Joy's spot. There was no use knocking as Joy was, for all intents and purposes, finished her normal bathroom routine, and the four kids had to share the bathroom.

But.

Joy's mom allowed Grandma to share her ensuite and Joy was allowed to use it 'only in emergencies'. The boys were banned. Joy's mom said they lost the privilege when they couldn't keep their aim. Joy had no idea what that meant.

Whatev', this was an emergency.

Joy tiptoed into her mom's room. She always found herself tiptoeing when she entered her mom's private space. There was something that warranted . . . caution and respect.

She pushed the sliding bathroom door open and stood in front of the sink. Time was ticking. Unscrewing the lid, she poured a few grains of the coffee crystals into her hand, adjusted the water to a trickle . . . and quickly flicked some water into the open palm. The coffee dissolved almost immediately into a dark brown mess. Working quickly, she put her index finger in the mixture, giving it a stir, and then brought her stained finger up and across her pale brow.

IT WORKED!

Satisfied, she did the other one.

"BOOM!" she said to her own reflection.

Joy looked as if she had slept for days. No longer did she look pale and sickly. She actually had definition to her flat face. And, as she turned her face left and right, Joy thought her new eyebrows made her nose look a bit smaller too.

She washed her hands quickly. A slight stain remained on her finger and in her hand.

Joy rushed, walking a bit faster to school having spent so much time in her mom's bathroom admiring her new self. The warning bell rang when she was still a half a block away, so she broke out into a trot. Her three friends were waiting for her at the front of the school and were waving her in.

"Joy, you're never the last one," Ava said as they squeezed in through the front double doors together, "Wait. Something is different about you? You look . . . surprised or something?"

Sally and Sofia both tilted their heads, giving Joy the up and down and all around look over.

Joy's cheeks began to glow.

Shrugging her shoulders, Sofia held up an envelope, "Look what I've got!"

All three girls giggled with glee. The final bell rang and they were technically in the classroom, but not in their desks. Joy grabbed the envelope and gave Sofia a high five, as they all dispersed and slid into their designated seats.

Joy tried to act normal, but her insides were turning. It wasn't Holy Spirit, it was . . . odd. She closed her eyes and checked herself. It wasn't a stinky weed emotion . . . it was . . . anticipation!

Joy's life was looking good. She had eyebrows AND the secret photos!

Jan, the leader of the cool girls group, flicked a tiny paper ball onto Joy's desk during second period when Ms. Sinclair was busy writing a dividing fractions equation on the board. Placing the note in her lap, Joy carefully unraveled it. There, written in purple glitter were the words:

nice eybrows!
you should totes
where maskara!
Jan
xo

Joy smiled. Jan wasn't the best speller in fifth grade, but she was the most popular girl. All the boys stared at her. Not just because she wore makeup, but also because she . . . well . . . she didn't have a third grade body like Joy.
Joy wadded up the paper, looked over to Jan and smiled.
At least someone noticed her new look.

Chapter 10

The girls huddled together on the roof club meeting spot at lunch, the three naturally dark eye-browed girls still having not noticed Joy's big breakthrough. Only a fellow natural pale blonde like Jan could appreciate what a big deal it was to finally not have a flat face.

"Joy, open it!" Sally said, nudging Joy.

Joy looked at Sofia, "Have you looked at them yet?"

"Yeah, I helped mom put them in the envelope."

"Weeeelllll?" the three other girls looked intently at Sofia who was busy shoving her sandwich into her mouth.

Sofia's shoulders rose so high, they almost touched her ears, "I donno," she muffled through a full mouth, "a bunch of boring people? None of your family."

Joy took a dramatic deep breath, closed her eyes and prayed, "Father God, whatever is in here, make it . . . interesting!"

Snickers and giggles broke out in the tight, small circle.

Ava placed her arm around Joy to show her support . . . and leaned in to have a good vantage as Joy slowly flipped the flap open.

Before Joy saw anything, Sofia spoke again, "Mom said a lot of the photos were trash cuz the film was so old, but she managed to develop a few of them."

As Joy pulled out the photos, strips of brown clear plastic fell out and into her lap. "What are these weird things?" she asked holding them up.

"Those are called the negatives. They are kinda cool."

Joy shoved them back into the envelope and held the group of photos to her chest. Before she looked at them, she counted them, "one, two, three, four, five, six . . . seven."

Sofia rolled her eyes and scrunched up her nose, "Oh Joy Bomb, why must you count all the time?"

Joy laughed with them. It was a quirky thing, she knew that.

"Okay, here we go!" Joy said as she held the photos at a distance so her friends could see with her.

Sally scooted along the warm asphalt tile roof to the other side of Joy, while Sofia having already seen the pictures, continued to scarf down her sandwich.

The first photo was of a Christmas tree.

"Boring!" Joy said, placing it at the back of the bunch.

The next picture had a bunch of fancy dressed people crowded together at a banquet table, with a horrible glitter covered holly and candy cane center piece.

"Tacky Christmas!" Ava said.

Joy nodded in agreement, searching the faces. None of them looked familiar.

They moved on to picture number three, only to find it was almost exactly like the second . . . and the fourth . . . and the fifth.

"Ugh!" Joy said exasperated. "Why are there four pictures almost exactly the same?"

Sofia looked up and stopped chewing. She pushed her half-chewed sandwich into the corner of her cheek, making herself look like a deranged chipmunk. "Mom said people used to do that all the time. The old cameras didn't have screens like our phones or real cameras like we, um, well like some of us have today. So they took a whole bunch of shots, just to make sure they got a good one."

The girls looked at each other, somewhat confused.

"Like Jan taking selfies!" Sally said, laughing as she slapped her knee. Ava and Sofia snickered along with her.

"That's not nice!" Joy said.

The three girls stared at their friend, wondering why she would defend the girl who – just a few weeks ago – slammed Joy in the head on purpose during a Phys. Ed. game of dodge ball.

"Just because some people care about how they look, doesn't mean you should make fun of them!" Joy finished.

The four of them sat quietly, none of them speaking or moving. Even the bulge in Sofia's cheek didn't dare budge.

Joy looked at her three besties. She looked down at picture five of the group of strangers. Were they still friends? They were all smiling and cozy in the photo. Do people stay close like that forever? Her stomach clenched. Shoving the pictures back into the envelope, she didn't even care what the last two pictures showed.

She dropped the package into her lunch bag, zipped it closed, and quietly spoke over the roof tiles that were at her chin as she stood on the third rung of the rope ladder, "At least Jan noticed my new eyebrows."

Ava slapped her forehead and said to the remaining girls, "Her eyebrows! I knew there was something different!"

But by then, Joy was long gone.

Joy ran all the way home, without reporting to the office or asking for a dismissal note. She came crashing in the front door just as Grandma came out of the kitchen, wiping her hands on her apron.

"Joy Amelia Bomb, what on earth are you doing home so early?" Grandma Joyce asked. "And what did you do to your eyebrows?"

Joy burst into tears and ran to her room, with her grandmother in hot pursuit behind her.

"Joy, what on earth happened?" her grandmother's hand gently rubbed Joy's shoulders and upper back as the girl sobbed into her pillow. "Did someone hurt you? Touch you?"

Flipping onto her back, Joy looked at her grandmother, "Why is that almost always the first thing you and mom ask? Steve and Billy punch me all the time in the arm, but you never care about that!"

She flipped back over onto her pillow.

"Did you punch someone again?" Joyce Neil asked, recalling the unfortunate, Sally-Floor-Flattening event that had happened the month before.

"UGH! NO!" Joy yelled after she turned over again.

"Listen young lady, you will not yell at me unless the house is on fire . . . again . . ."

That made them both laugh a bit, easing Joy's pain.

"I am going to call the school before they lock it down and think you've been abducted." Joyce got out her cell and Joy admired the big full screen. Even her old grandmother was cooler than her.

As Joyce waited for the phone to be answered she said to Joy, "Once we tell the school to stand down, you are going to tell me what on earth is going on!"

"Hello? Yes, this is Joy Bomb's grandmother calling. I just want to let you know that Joy is at home with me. Pardon me? Oh my word, since when is that necessary? I am one of her caregivers."

Joyce Neil held the phone out to Joy, "They need to speak with you to confirm you are okay."

Joy took the sleek phone into her hand. It felt good and legit. Not like the flimsy fuchsia flip phone she was forced to use. "Hello? Yes, this is me. What?"

Joyce Neil nudged her granddaughter.

"I mean, pardon me," Joy corrected herself. "Yes, I know I was supposed to ask before coming home, but . . . um . . . I started to feel kinda sick when I was eating my lunch," Joy said. It wasn't really a lie.

"What? Um, I mean pardon me? Um, NO! It is not THAT!" Joy said sternly. Why do people always assume every fifth grade girl who is not feeling well is going through the change of life?

"Yes. You are probably right," Joy looked at her grandmother as a smile finally broke through her tears, "It probably was something my grandmother cooked and put in my lunch."

Grandma Joyce's cell began to buzz in Joy's hand, so she quickly handed it back to her. The caller ID was for a hair salon. "Hello, I'm sorry, I have to go, I have a call coming through and I am late for an appointment! Yes, I'm sorry about that. I will have a good talk with Joy and she won't do this again if I have any say. No, of course not. I will not be leaving Joy alone unsupervised."

Joy lay on the sofa at Mrs. Solomon's house as her neighbor crashed about in the kitchen, "Mrs. S?" Joy called out. "I feel fine. I don't need to lie down and I'd rather be helping you."

Gwen Solomon poked her head out of the kitchen and looked at Joy, "I told your grandmother you wouldn't have any fun. And as such, you will lie there until you are so bored, your brains fall out."

Sighing, Joy decided now was as good as time as ever to try and interface with God. She didn't have her prayer journal, but she also knew she didn't need it to pray.

She closed her eyes and silently asked Holy Spirit, the Spirit of Truth, to calm her crazy thoughts so she could hear God. Joy decided to use one of her favorite names of God, YAHWEH, to address him. Joy thought it was amazing that God had dozens of different names. Mrs. S had told her that just like she sometimes would call her mom, 'mother', 'mom' or 'mommy' depending on her request, Jesus followers can also talk to their Heavenly Father with special names for different needs. But today, she thought YAHWEH was a good one to use as it means, 'He brings into existence whatever exists'; or can also mean, 'He is'! Joy needed God to bring something into existence in her life.

Folding her hands, Joy began to whispery pray, "YAHWEH, my God that brings all things into existence. You already know what I am going to ask for, but I am going to ask anyhow, just so there is no confusion. Father God, could you pleeeeeeaase get me a tube of mascara? In Jesus' name, Amen."

Joy looked at the wall clock. Only five minutes had passed since she prayed. It wasn't even 2pm yet and she was told she had to 'stay put' until her regular home from school time, 3:15pm.

"Mrs. S?" Joy called from the couch, "I need to use the washroom. Is that allowed?"

The older neighbor ducked her head out again, "Yes, but no dilly-dallying. Just do your business and get back to the couch."

"Dilly-dallying?" Joy whispered to herself. She hadn't heard that since preschool when Mrs. Solomon used to babysit her. Standing in front of the mirror, Joy was pleased to see that her eyebrows still had a very subtle tint of brown to them. She tilted her head admiring the unflattness of her new face.

"Joy Bomb, are you dillying?"

"No, I'm dallying" Joy yelled back through the door, laughing.

"Joy!"

"I'm . . ." Joy quickly sat on the toilet, "on the toilet!"

Joy felt a burning in her chest and a tightness in her belly. She knew she hadn't technically lied to her mentor, but it still wasn't right. She decided she probably did have some pee in her so she whipped her pants down and made proper use of her time. As she sat there, she decided to pray again.

* * *

"Father God? Am I allowed to pray to you when I am . . . um . . . doing this?" she giggled. "Well, I'm sorry for kinda lying to Mrs. S. Please don't hold it against me and not give me my mascara. Amen."

Satisfied that she had properly undone her little white lie by actually using the toilet, not just sitting on it, Joy flushed and washed her hands. Turning a bit too quickly, Joy knocked the little wooden sign by the sink onto the floor.

If you sprinkle when you tinkle, Be a sweetie & wipe the seatie!

Joy read quietly as she picked it up. It was kinda kitschy, but it made her smile.

As she stood to return the sign to its spot, there, right on the floor between the toilet and the garbage can was a glimmering gold tube of . . . black mascara.

God had answered her prayers!

Hello God? Can I tell You something...

Wow! You DO LOVE ME! I mean, You are up to something. Jan told me to get mascara, and then You provided.

Yahweh Jireh — Your name that means You provide for me. Ya got that right! You're amazing.
It's so beautiful. Is it real gold?

Thanks once again for taking a real poopy day and making it good.

Today I feel

Gratitude and Thanks

*MY DREAM COME TRUE! MY OWN MASCARA!

I hear what I think You MAY be saying, but I don't like it.
It was in the garbage. Well, it was supposed to be in the bin, but Mrs. S missed it.

What is God saying to me about this?

Father, maybe I should have asked her and not just taken it, but . . . I really, really wanted it and then she may have told mom, or made me ask her if I was allowed. Mom wouldn't understand what it is like to have no eyelashes or eyebrows.

The Bible says You cover me with grace (forgiveness), so even if I might have made a mistake, You will work it all out for me.

I mean, what can go wrong?

Since You're listening, I kinda need . . .

*Peace in my tummy.

Thank You for hearing & loving me!

Chapter 11

Joy turned off her alarm clock through blurry eyes. She had stayed up late practicing how to put on her new mascara.

A smile, brighter than the gold tube, lit up Joy's face. She folded her hands, took a few deep breaths and waited. Finally, once she felt she really had her mind on God and not the other junk that was flying around in her head, she began, "Father God, Dad, thanks SO much for this day, for Your help yesterday, and for being with me always. Today is a great day for a miracle through me and to me! In Jesus' name, amen!"

Tossing the blankets off, she grabbed her clean underwear and the clothes she had so carefully chosen the night before. Normally, since Joy was a bit of a tomboy, she didn't really care about fashion but would grab whichever t-shirt that was the least stinky off the pile of laundry on her floor. But, today was THE day. Joy had thought she would have to wait until she started Middle school in three months to recreate herself, but she was happy to get a jump start. She reached under her bed where she had stashed the small bag with a container of coffee crystals and the new shiny gift from her Heavenly Dad.

The bathroom was empty so she had a quick shower, even using soap under her pits, and toweled off before one of her brothers started to bang on the door.

She was glad it wasn't a hair wash day so she could take her time unflattening her face. Brushing her long, blonde, poker-straight locks, she put a small clip on both sides of her hair so that her new face could be seen. Her forehead looked ultra-square like that though, so she parted her hair a bit off center and tried again. Much better.

Next she opened the crystals and tapped a few into her hand. Always one to try new things, she decided to add a bit of the moisturizer by the sink that the boys used to shave with to make a paste instead of water. It had worked well last night and did not disappoint this morning.

With eyebrows nicely visible, Joy took the gold tube she had found and rolled it between her fingers like a magician does with cards. It glittered in the bathroom light as it flew back and forth.

"Who's in there?" a groggy Billy banged on the door.

"Two more minutes!" Joy answered. Her heart was pounding. She put the tube down, put on the top her mom had bought her for her work Christmas party, and her best pair of jeans. She looked good, but not so good that it looked like she was trying. On the front of her shirt was a heart made of sequins. She flipped them up, and it was pink. If she flipped them all down, a rainbow heart would appear.

BANG-BANG-BANG!

"One more minute!" Joy hollered.

"I'm so glad I practiced this last night," she said quietly. She applied the black smudgy goo onto her left eyelashes without much of a problem, but her right eye kept flickering and was blurry. Her hand began to shake and she hit her cheek a few times, but managed to get both eyes to match.

• • •

She stood back, tilted her head back and forth admiring the dimensions her face had now. Her nose was definitely looking smaller.

Joy packed up her secret stash, and turned to leave. Suddenly, she noticed her belly had been fluttering. She stopped, picked the wet towel up off the floor and hung it.

"Father God . . . um . . . ABBA Father . . . Dad . . ." she said, unsure of what exactly to call Him today, "You sure like to tell me what to do!"

Joy walked slowly to school. She wanted her walk to look more relaxed and fashionable, rather than her normal sloppy, trippy, frantic rushed gait. She felt herself slouching with the weight of her backpack, so she pushed her shoulders back, and straightened her posture. That made her flat chest stick out though, so she decided to take the backpack and swing it over one shoulder, the way Jan's group of girls does. That felt better. It felt more . . . middle schoolish.

Her arm began to ache as she neared the school. She ignored the pain and concentrated hard on keeping her steps looking effortless and graceful.

That was when it happened.

Just as she turned the final corner that brought her to the school's street, Joy walked full on hard into someone. Her backpack slipped of her shoulder, and one of her hairclips got hooked on the man's sweater.

Apologizing, but also mad that this man had just ruined Joy's graceful approach, she wondered if any of the students from Spruce Gardens Elementary were witnessing her misfortune.

"Here, don't move, you are ruining my sweater!" the man said crossly. "Stop pulling away, your clip is making a big snag on my new cashmere pullover!" He said a tad louder.

But Joy didn't care about some dumb fancy sweater. She just wanted to go back around the corner and get away from the watchful eyes of Spruce Garden elementary students. Once she got out of sight, she could fix her hair, take a few deep breaths, and attempt a take two on her new willowy walk.

Joy took five steps backwards, and the stranger kept stepping along with her. It was like some weird awkward backwoods tribal dance as Joy managed to lead them both around the corner, and out of the school's view.

"WAIT!" Joy yelled. "Move your hand so I can unhook my clip."

The man let go of the clip.

Joy pinched the sides together and it opened, releasing the precious fibers of his oh-so-fancy sweater.

Finally detached, Joy mumbled a half-hearted apology, never actually looking at the stranger. She put her backpack on her left shoulder this time, and after confidently flipping her loose hair over her back, began to walk casually but calculatedly towards a new life with her new identity.

Perhaps it was the unscheduled rendezvous with Mr. Fancy Pants, or maybe it was her new popular girl, graceful stride that took longer than her normal clumsy half-trot, but even though Joy had left earlier, she arrived just as the warning bell was ringing. Her friends were nowhere to be seen so she entered the school alone. She settled herself into her seat, very self-conscious of her unflat face. She was actually relieved not to have encountered anyone.

As Ms. Sinclair began the normal morning routine, Joy could sense people were looking at her. She wasn't sure what she should do. Who knew trying to be popular and play it cool was so hard on a person? How on earth has Jan been doing it for so long?

Just as Joy was about to pull out her math book, a wad of paper hit her desk like an accurate, secret mission missile. Unraveling it, Joy smiled to see the familiar purple glitter ink.

'Wow! You totes lisened to me and got the maskara! You look amaxsing. Sit with me at lunch.
Your bestie,
Jan xoxo'

Joy looked over at the missile launcher. Jan's perfectly groomed eyebrows were high, her eyes big and dramatic with layers of eyeshadow, and her smile, HUGE. And, she was giving Joy not one . . . but TWO thumbs up.

A note like that was typical Jan. Grammar and spelling errors galore. Plus, Jan never asked anyone to do anything. She told them what to do.

Joy was in.

Joy was in with the popular girls club. Just. Like. That. One tube of mascara was all that was needed. Who knew?

Joy knew. She always knew that makeup would change her life forever!

Joy sat taller in her seat than she had ever done, having received the life-altering note. A positive note from Jan could elevate her even higher than the Sally-floor-flattening event. Joy felt her face flush. She used to despise Sally, but after Joy bopped her in the nose after Christmas, the two girls got to know each other and became super close. Joy pondered . . . she took a pencil and began to doodle.

Joy erased her thought. She gently blew the pink dust off the book and with her hand made a pile on the corner of her desk. She tried again.

From the corner of her eye, Joy saw Jan doodling in her notebook, erasing, and then, to Joy's amazement, the coolest girl in fifth grade neatly pinched a bunch of pink eraser dust and started her own pile on the corner of her desk.

She looked over at Joy and smiled, giving her an 'okay' signal with her fingers.

Joy was not only in with the most popular girls group, Joy was INFLUENCING the most popular girl in fifth grade!

Chapter 12

Joy walked into her house. The day had been . . . dreamy. Even the drizzly rain while walking home couldn't dampen her mood. She took a seat on their welcome bench and pulled out her butterfly book as she sat reflecting on the glorious day.

She had sat with the popular girls at lunch for two days now, and they all swooned over her sequined top and kept telling her how pretty she was, now that she wore makeup. Joy wore the same top for two days, as it was the only girly one she had. Jan told her after school when they chatted at the bike racks that wearing the same outfit twice in one week was not acceptable. And definitely not two days in a row. She said because Joy was new in the group, she would let it go, but Joy needed to be careful to follow their fashion rules.

The rest of the group asked to see her pink dust collection and all of her new friends found containers of some sort to collect their own eraser sprinkles. At each health break and afterschool, they would compare their levels. It became a competition of sorts to see who could accumulate more. Of course, Jan's mom bought her erasers of different colors that had glitter in them. Her dust looked amazing, but didn't have that unique smell Joy loved, nor did it feel good to rub between fingers. Joy didn't tell them what she wrote or why she did what she did. But, they never asked anyhow.

It was a bit awkward, having to ditch her regular friends.

Joy wasn't sure if they were confused or mad, but it didn't matter. Joy had a plan. She was going to lead the cool girls to Jesus, and then unite her old group of friends with her new group. Her old friends would be so THANKFUL that she got them into the popular group. But first, she had to play it cool and blend in with the new girls for a while. It wouldn't take long and the Fab Four would be the Fab Eight.

She had gotten better at getting the mascara on this morning, but her right eye did still twitch and feel itchy. Joy made sure she wiped off the makeup after school before going home. Someday she would ask her mom, but with all the stress and whispers at home lately, she decided it was better to ask forgiveness later, than for permission right now.

She bit her lip. She knew that probably wasn't right, but it felt so good to finally not be the most awkward, clumsy, flat-faced girl in fifth grade.

She opened her small notebook and began to write.

Was it my imagination, or was Jan being mean to Lisa at lunch?

They had their own group of four and Joy made it five. Joy rubbed out what she had written and then added.

I think Jan may ditch Lisa to make room for me?

As she took her time rubbing out her depressing thought, her mind wandered . . . she remembered the video they had watched in science class about baby chicks and how there is always a 'pecking order'. The weakest, smallest chick . . . Joy shuddered. Her hand went down to her belly, it didn't feel great. A knot began to form in her throat. She decided to write again.

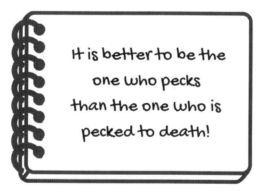

It is better to be the one who pecks than the one who is pecked to death!

And then madly, feverishly, she wiped it out.
"Joy," her Grandma Joyce called from the kitchen, "Where have you been? We are sitting down for dinner."

Shaking off the melancholy, she made her way into the kitchen. Robert was home for dinner, and Mom, Grandma and Billy were crowded around the small table, already ripping apart the deli-roasted chicken. Burning up the stove was an answer to Joy's prayers. They ate a lot of pizza, Chinese and deli now.

Normally, Joy loved the rotisserie chicken, but having just recalled the nasty, graphic science lesson, and with her tummy still in a knot, Joy reached for the salad instead and placed her bowl on a spot at the island.

She examined the various salad dressings on the table, checking expiration dates before she settled on the freshest which happened to be the ranch. The four at the table were all talking and grabbing at food like they hadn't eaten in days. Sitting alone at the island, her back to her family, Joy muttered, "So uncivilized," soft enough for no one else to hear.

"What's this? I'm finally home for a family dinner and my baby sister won't eat with us?" Robert said. There was levity in his voice but Joy also heard a touch of sadness.

She picked up her salad bowl and stood. Billy's wheelchair was huge and took up a lot of room.

Seeing her eyes searching around the table, Billy placed his plate in his lap and pulled his wheelchair away a few feet. He was close enough to join the conversation, but he had opened up an empty space. He gave a dramatic wave, as if having just done some amazing illusion. The siblings smiled at each other.

"For you, my favorite sister," he quipped.

"I'm your only sister, Bog-Boy," making a fist to slug her brother in his arm like they always did, Joy caught herself and dropped her hand . . . like a lady.

"Well, we always make room for the ones we love!" Billy said, giving his sister a wink.

Robert pushed a chair with his foot towards his sister, and Joy took a seat.

"So, Joy-Joy, what's new in your life?" Robert asked as he shoved an entire heavily-buttered, sweet bun into his mouth.

"Oh, not much," Joy said. She knew enough to keep her newfound popularity a secret.

"No?" Robert said, laughing.

Joy looked at her brother, then her mother, and lastly her Grandma Joyce. They were all snickering.

Heat rose into Joy's cheeks. She didn't like this feeling. Joy looked at her brother Billy, but he had his head down and was flat out laughing too.

"You know what?" Joy said, standing, "I am tired of always being the black sheep of this family!"

Billy looked at his sister, tears were falling he was laughing so hard, "Well, I don't know about you being the black sheep, but you sure do have two black eyes!"

Joy's black eyes grew large. She looked at her mom to see if today was going to be her last day on earth, but her mom and grandma were holding hands and laughing their heads off.

Robert rose from the table, and put his arms around his sister. He was so tall, Joy was practically staring into his bellybutton.

"Joy, you can do whatever you want with those pretty blue eyes of yours, but I just want you to know from a guy's point of view, you are a very pretty girl and you don't need that paint."

Joy stood as stiff as a board. She didn't know if she wanted to return his hug or slug him. But, at least with his bear hug, she didn't have to face her mom. She didn't slug or hug, but rather decided a limp doll stance would be her best defense and, as such, let her body get floppy as if she fainted.

Robert let go of his sister without any warning, and Joy hit the floor. With the prowess of a cat, as soon as her butt hit the hard tiled floor, she flipped herself into a backwards roll, and kept rolling, until she was out of her family's keen eyes.

Finally, all Joy's clumsy falls were paying off as she executed one of her best exits ever.

Hello God? Can I tell You something...

Tumbling thoughts tonight, God. Are You sure You know what You are doing with my life?

I mean, I think You placed me in the cool group to influence them, but tonight was SO EMBARASSING. Even if it was just my family.

Why would You give me mascara, only to have it melt on my face in the rain?

I thought I had gotten it all washed off?

Good news, mom said she would help me find some age appropriate lip gloss. No more coffee in her bathroom (did you know it stains white towels?) I guess You would know since You created everything.

Today I feel

Gratitude and Thanks

*that my mom was so cool

I know. This feeling in my tummy has been talking for days. I am SO confused though.

What is God saying to me about this?

Is this what You meant when You said life was going to get bumpy?
I remember Grandma Joyce and Mrs. S talking about people who leave their family and friends to share Jesus. They were called hissionairies or something like that. Is the popular group where I am supposed to go?

Father, You say that when You send people places, it shouldn't cause me to be deceitful and hurt my friends or family.

You have big plans for me? Hello?! Wow! Oh, but I am not supposed to use the grace You gave me to be selfish, stubborn and rebellious. Gotcha.

Since You're listening, I kinda need . . .

*My eye to stop being so itchy

Thank You for hearing & loving me!

Chapter 13

Joy's mom sat on the edge of her bed, as she pulled on Joy's eyelids and looked into her eye.

"I don't know, Gumby, it isn't really red or anything."

Joy reached up to rub her eyes but her mother grabbed her wrist and stopped her.

"Where is that tube you found?" she asked her daughter.

Joy flipped herself over the edge of her bed, her long legs keeping her balance so she didn't head plant on the floor. She reached under her bed and pulled out the small bag. Flipping herself back up, her mother watched in disbelief.

"Oh to have your abs!" Helen Bomb said, sucking in her slightly squishy belly.

Laughing, Joy tossed the bag at her mother and twisted herself into a headstand.

"My daughter, the contortionist! You sure have lived up to your name!"

Helen looked at the tube, pulling it out and examining it. "It looks really old, Hon. You really need to ask Mrs. Solomon about this. You need to never, ever borrow your friends' makeup. Germs get shared and you could get infections. We will figure out what is age appropriate for you – not mascara – but we will help you feel less," Helen stifled a laugh, "less flat-faced. But again, never ever borrow makeup. I remember once in college, I borrowed my friend's eyeliner and-"

Joy cut off her mother, "You wore makeup?"

"Yes, Joy," Helen laughed, "I wasn't always a worn-out hag. Be sure to not ever use this again, and give it back to Mrs. Solomon."

Joy's chest began to burn, "Mom, don't say that about yourself. You are super pretty, but just in a plain, mom way."

Helen Bomb, looked down and began to anxiously straighten out her daughter's bed sheets, tucking them in tightly.

"Mom," Joy shoved her feet back under her covers, kicking them loose, "you know I don't like them constricted."

Helen sighed.

"Seriously Mom, it's like what Robert said to me, only it's true for you! You already have eyelashes and eyebrows." Joy knelt on her bed, looking her mom in the eyes. "You could pluck some of those eyebrows though. They look a bit bushy."

"When did you get to be an expert on eyebrows?" Helen asked,

"Sitting with the popular girls at school." Joy answered without thinking.

"Oh? Are your other friends sitting there too?"

Flopping back on her bed, Joy couldn't look at her mother, "No, I only sat with them for two days."

"Well, Gum, how do your friends feel about you ditching them?"

Joy smashed her pillow into her head, "I dunno. I haven't talked to them in a while."

"Oh, Joy," Helen pulled the pillow off and looked into her daughter's eyes. "I'll make a deal with you, you go talk to your friends at Mrs. Solomon's today and make things right, and . . . and I will go get my hair and eyebrows done."

* * *

Joy looked at her mom. Her dark hair was always straight and often pulled into a pony tail. Flecks of grey ran through it. Joy thought they were beautiful like tinsel from the Christmas tree, but her mom said they made her look old, and if she won the lottery, she would dye them. She must have won some money.

"Aren't you working today?" Joy asked as her mom walked out her bedroom door.

"Not today. We need to have a family talk after your group so be sure to come straight home. Do you hear me?"

"Yes ma'am." Joy reached over and grabbed her small notepad.

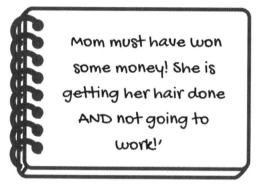

Mom must have won some money! She is getting her hair done AND not going to work!

She flopped back down into bed and began to daydream. What would life look like as millionaires?

Joy looked around her room. She felt like she had never thought about what was missing, but now that the possibilities were endless, she began to rethink her sparse surroundings.

She looked at the space by the closet, and held up her hands as if they were a frame, "A makeup table with lights could fit right there." Wait. They probably wouldn't be renting this house anymore, but would buy a mansion! Joy wondered if Sally's parents would sell them their house. It was the biggest, fanciest in town. Joy had only been there a few times. It smelled and sounded like a museum. When they walked down the hall, their footsteps echoed. Sally preferred to usually hang out at Joy's house and Joy agreed. But, with the Bomb boys filling up the place, the mansion would be more homey and less . . . like a law firm.

Joy imagined her brothers sliding down the polished wooden round bannisters, flying off at the end.

Suddenly, a long forgotten memory popped into her head. A fuzzy picture. She was in a hard plastic boat. She was little, maybe four years old? They were in a big house. Not Sally big, but bigger than the rancher they currently rented. The Bomb boys lifted the boat up onto the double railing over the stairs from the back deck down to the yard. And, once they had it balanced, they gave it a push. Joy and the boat flew down the railing at rocket speed . . . until the end . . . where the boat did not float to the ground, but fell with a hard thump. The memory caused Joy to jump.

She got her butterfly book.

Did that really happen? Was that a dream? Was that our house?

When Joy reached for her eraser, she saw the time on her bedside clock. She had to hurry to get to Mrs. Solomon's before her friends. Sharpening her pencil, thoughtfully, she wrote next to her last comment.

Did that really happen? Was that a dream? Was that our house?
Will the girls even show up?

Joy dusted the pink bits into her plastic cylinder and as she did, remembered the photos from Wednesday. After laying on Mrs. S's couch all afternoon, she was so excited to try the mascara, she dumped the contents of half-eaten food from her lunch bag into the garbage. Thankfully, before she ran up to open the golden tube, Joy fished the envelope out of the bin and tucked it somewhere safe.

"Think, think, think," Joy mumbled to herself as she paced her room. "Joy Amelia Bomb, where did you put it?"

Looking at the clock, she knew she had to go. She grabbed the mascara, her Fab Four notebook and Bible, and scooted out the door.

Joy arrived ten minutes early. It wasn't a lot of time, but she needed to give Mrs. S the scoop.

"Oh, Joy, you're a bit early, Hon. No Billy today?"

"No, he is hanging out with the Bog-Boys today."

The two neighbors looked at each other, "But not in my room!" Joy added

"Oh, that's too bad," the older lady said, "I have a basement that needs to be swept and cleared out."

"Mrs. S, I need to tell you something." Joy slid in her hand into her back pocket and pulled out the gold tube of mascara, "I found this on your bathroom floor the other day, and I . . . took it."

"Oh dear. Oh no, Joy," concern etched across her face. "I threw that out as it was so old."

Joy scrunched up her mouth, "I'm sorry; I should have asked to have it and then you could have told me."

"Is that why you came early? So you could come clean?"

"Well, there was that," Joy's toes crossed over her other foot, and curled around them. "Well, with my face being less flat-"

"Pardon me?" the neighbor interrupted Joy.

"My face looks flat without eyebrows and eyelashes. Anyhow, with my face looking better, the popular girls at school asked me to be friends and eat lunch with them. I decided I could like, hang out with them, and tell them about Jesus. They totally like me. They even copy the way I collect eraser guts."

"Eraser guts?" the old lady looked confused. "Listen Joy, what about your real friends? Sally, Sofia and Ava? Were they invited to hang out with you?"

Looking down at the worn area rug under her toes, Joy took a deep breath, "No. They weren't."

"What did your new friends think about your spiritual life?"

Joy began to flick the corner of the rug with her toes. "I haven't told them yet. I thought I needed to go slowly."

The older lady gently placed her hands on Joy's knee, "So tell me, my Joy Bomb, do I put out five glasses of lemonade today, or two?" The older lady rose and made her way into the kitchen, "I can smell the cookies are ready," and as she said it, the oven timer began to chime.

Tears began to well up in Joy's eyes. She reached into her pocket and pulled out the small pencil and book.

I have ruined everything

As she rubbed it out, Joy heard the sound of pounding hooves on the front deck. Mrs. S poked her head out from the kitchen, a big smile across her face. "Can you let your friends in, dear?"

The girls sat quietly munching on cookies. Mrs. Solomon looked through her playlist, praying. She chose a slow song, "Okay girls, how about if I open in prayer today."

The girls nodded in silent unity.

"Father God, we thank You that we know You hear us. As we gather here together, we take authority over this room and we cleanse it – along with our own imaginations of any nefarious thoughts or spirits and only welcome Your angels and YOU, Holy Spirit, The Spirit of Truth, to join us. In Jesus' name we pray, Amen"

The girls looked at their spiritual mentor. The room, prayer or not, still felt dark and smudgy, like Joy Bomb's black, mascara-running eyes had been.

"All right. You four need to talk, and you don't need an old lady hovering over you." Mrs. Solomon slapped her thighs and raised up with an "ooof" groan. "I'll be on the back porch if you need me."

Joy sat staring at the floor, wishing her ally was still with them. She could sense three sets of eyes burrowing into her brain.

Finally, Ava spoke, "So, is Jesus popular enough for you?"

Joy looked up, "That's rude."

"Oh, so ignoring your friends is not rude?" Sofia said.

"Ya," Sally said, in her short, careful what you say way.

A weird crackling sound filled Joy's ears. She swallowed hard, and cleared her throat, "I admit. I was . . . a . . . nasty stinkweed."

Sofia snickered, "Ya, that sums it up nicely."

"Why, Joy? Why? Do you like them more than us?" Ava said. "I mean I know I used to blow you guys off, but that was before I made a choice to follow God's spiritual path for me."

Joy looked at her friends. Sally refused to look at her, Ava was glaring through tears, and Sofia, sweet Sofia, was focused on a cookie that she was slowly crumbling into her lap.

"I'm sorry. I was wrong." It was rare for Joy to speak plainly. She tended to use humor to avoid conflict.

"So, what's it going to be, Joy? Are you going to keep ignoring us to be with them?" Ava asked, her arms crossed.

Joy stopped and put her hand on her tummy. She knew what she had to do. "Okay, on Monday we will ALL go to their table and sit down. We are a group. We are meant to stay connected. If they want me, they have to take all of us!"

"Joy Bomb, that mascara leaked into your brain. That is not a good idea. We will be socially destroyed," Sally said.

Shrugging her shoulders, Joy took a bite of a cookie, "So, we will all die together!"

Chapter 15

Joy and Sally sat on the edge of Joy's bed. "Thanks for coming to help me, Sally." Joy said.

"Well, it was either come here to help you find your missing photos or stay home and watch our domestic helper polish the silver. Again." Sally rolled her eyes. "Is your grandma making dinner?"

"No," Joy giggled, "I'm sorry you can't stay for dinner. Actually, we have to be fast because mom said we have some kid of big family meeting." Joy leaned close to her friend, "I think we won the lottery!"

Sally suddenly looked nervous, "I better go."

"No, not yet! You've got to help me."

"Fine," Sally was looking over her shoulder as if expecting to be interrupted or to see a ghost or something. "Let's retrace your steps. Tell me exactly what you did."

"Okay, I came home from Mrs. S's, ran into the kitchen, dumped out the gross food into the garbage can . . . and then saw the envelope under the banana peel. I fished it out, and . . . that's all I can remember!"

"Don't freak out," Sally said sternly, "That is never productive. That's what my parents always say to each other when they are working on a case. Think. You were in the kitchen. Where did you go to next?"

Joy put her head into her hands, "I . . . came up here to try and put on the mascara."

"In your room?"

"No, in . . . the bathroom!"

Both girls jumped up and ran into the washroom. They closed the door behind them. "Think, Joy!" Sally whispered.

Joy stood with her hands out in front of her, as if she was about to run a sprint. "I . . . " she knelt down and opened a lower cabinet. She lifted a woven basket that was full of half-empty shampoo bottles. "Stuck it under here!"

Joy held up the envelope.

"Score!"

"Joy? Is that you in there?" Helen Bomb's voice sounded tense.

"Yeah, Sally is too." Joy said as she opened the door. "Mom, your hair looks amazing! I love that style and the color is perfect."

Nervous and a bit self-conscious, Helen smoothed out her new hairdo with her hand and a soft smile covered her face. She reached out and gave Sally a hug, "Oh, you are a sight for sore eyes! I'm so glad you are hanging around here again. No, Joy, we have to have a talk. Sally, you understand, I hope."

Sally nodded, gave a weak smile and took off without saying goodbye.

"Well, that was a swift exit," Helen said, "What's that you've got there?" pointing to the envelope.

Joy wasn't sure she wanted to tell her mom, but also didn't want to keep secrets. "Can I show you later? I'm kinda excited to hear your big news."

"Okay. We are waiting for Steve. Meet us in the family room in ten minutes."

Nodding, Joy couldn't take her eyes off her new mom. It was a shocking change. She wondered what people would think when she went to work on Monday.

Dashing into her room, Joy fished out a magnifying glass and sat on her bed. She opened the envelope and quickly turned to picture number six. It was a picture of a very pretty woman in a bright red dress, with lipstick that matched perfectly. She flipped to picture seven.

It was the same woman, sitting with a man this time, giving him a kiss on the cheek. And the man was . . . Joy's chest got tight . . . it was Joy's dad. Joy hadn't seen any pictures of her dad in a long time, but she knew it was him.

The photo was old. Like, really old. Before Joy was even born, old.

"Joy, we are waiting for you!" her mother's voice made Joy jump.

Joy shoved the photos back into the envelope and put it in her desk drawer.

"Coming!"

Joy slid down the hall, and shifting her feet, managed to direct her skid right into the family room, landing on the couch.

All the Bomb's stared at her, and she knew they were impressed. It was a rare talent.

Helen Bomb paced back and forth in front of the fireplace. "Okay, so you know ever since I got a hold of your dad the night Billy was in surgery, he's been pretty insistent on getting involved in your lives again."

"Wait," Joy interrupted already, "What? No, I didn't know that."

"Joy, you were right next to me. We texted back and forth. And you were there in the kitchen when grandma and I were talking about it last Saturday."

Joy stared at her brothers. There was no shock on their faces. She looked at Grandma Joyce who had a very tense face and was knitting so fast and tight, her fingers were turning red.

"What do you mean he wants to be around us more?" Joy said. "Did you sell us back to him?"

The boys started to laugh, "It's not funny!" Joy screamed, stomping her foot in protest.

"No, Gumby. Nobody is being sold. Your dad and I have talked a lot, and he said Billy's fall was a wakeup call for him. He realized how wrong he was to move away and never stay in touch. He and his . . ." Helen's voice cracked, "He and his new family have bought the old Frenchie house. He moved here to have relationship with you all. He regrets not having contact."

Joy kicked off her slippers in protest.

"Why doesn't anyone tell me anything around here?"

"Joy, wait," Helen moved towards her daughter.

"Everyone leave me alone!" Joy took off barefoot through the front door at a full run. She knew where the Frenchie house was. They had moved away almost a year before. She crossed the street, then took a shortcut down the lane. The same lane Joy and Sofia walk back and forth between their homes. The road between their two streets was where the Frenchies used to live. The house that had been dark for months, was now lit up.

Joy stopped and crouched down in front of a tidy white picket fence that marked the home's front yard.

* * *

As her hand reached to the ground to steady her stance, it landed on something hard. She picked it up. The rock in her hand felt heavy and cold, much like her heart. Through tears, Joy could see the laughing blonde family through a very clean, clear window as they sat in their living room.

"You want contact, Dad?" Joy cried as she clenched the rock.

Suddenly, Holy Spirit moved in her belly. *'Don't do it. I have plans for this.'*

Joy looked long and hard at the large stone that filled her hand. And then back at the perfect-picture window. The windows at her home had never looked so flawless . . . ever. Not the glass nor the people behind them.

Joy let her bottom hit the dirt, and wrapped her arms around her thin bare legs that were in front of her, the rock still in her hand as she debated what to do next.

"Joy?" a man's voice called out in the darkness, "Joy are you out there? Your mom called me. She's worried about you."

Joy didn't move but her hand tightened around the stone. She could see a man – her dad she supposed – standing on the front stoop.

Behind her, she could hear the sound of her brothers talking, their voices getting louder as the distance between them narrowed.

"There she is," Billy said, "Push me faster!"

"Squirt, don't make me chase after you. You stay put!" Steve said.

Joy obeyed. Just hearing their voices made her feel safe again.

She began to count the white pickets that were in between each post. She only had two sections counted before her brothers circled behind her.

Joy stood up and faced her siblings, but they were all looking behind her, their eyes on the house. She turned around to see what had her brothers so captivated.

"Kids, why don't you all come in for a bit? Sometimes unplanned visits work out to be the best." The man said.

Behind him stood a woman with a baby on her hip, wearing bright, red . . . lipstick.

The stone made a THUD as it hit the ground at Joy's feet.

Hello God? Can I tell You something...

Well, after almost six years I saw my dad tonight. I know You were there, but I wanted to write it here to remember.
Why did we all just stand at the gate like that stunned? Even Robert didn't move.
Billy of course finally found his tongue and was his normal charming self . . . he had dad eating out of his hand.

I am really confused about the woman in the picture. How could she have been with dad when he was so young? And now too?

Dad looked really . . . nervous. Robert looked like he might deck dad in the nose, but did stick his hand out and shook dad's hand. Steve said nothing. Not. A. Peep.

And, seriously. Another brother? You couldn't give me a half-sister?

Today I feel

Gratitude and Thanks

*That my brothers were with me

*Maybe thanks for Dad?

You are an interesting God. I'm calling You God again as Father seems . . . more confusing now.

What is God saying to me about this?

You are reminding me how mad I was at Billy, but then how good things got once I forgave him. And how my guts don't like it when I stuff hatred and unforgiveness down.

I really don't want to let nasty stink weeds grow in me, but then again, I think when it came to my dad running off with someone else and leaving us kids, those weeds maybe as stubborn as the one that gave Mrs. S such a bad time.

Sigh. I know You love me. I know in some weird universe he loves me too. Or he will. Maybe? He sure yelled though when I ruined his sweater.

Since You're listening, I kinda need . . .

*To help dad get the snag out of his sweater

Thank You for hearing & loving me!

Chapter 16

The girls sat in a circle on Sally's bedroom floor. An untouched bag of ketchup potato chips got passed around and around, but no eyes or stomachs were hungry. Sally passed Sofia an unopened package of gummy worms and Ava a bar of chocolate crispies; both the girls' favorites. But out of respect for their grieving friend, they dropped the intact treats onto the floor in front of them.

A silent vigil can't be rushed.

Eventually, Joy reached out and shoved some potato chips into her mouth as if giving a signal to her friends they were released to start munching.

The hush was comforting, not only to Joy, but also to her friends. There is something peaceful about joining a friend in her pain, without trying to fix it. Crinkles of wrappers and soft munches took the edge off the stillness.

"I just want you guys to know, I get that you kinda tried to tell me, but I wasn't willing to listen." Joy finally spoke, accidently spraying chips across the floor. The grossness broke the tension.

Stifled giggles escaped hands that were clasped tight against faces.

"I know I'm only eleven, but I am still held to lawyers' kids – client privilege. I think. Anyhow, I heard my parents talking and, let's face it, a name like 'Bomb' kind of catches your attention," Sally said.

The girls giggled, even Joy joined in.

"It wasn't really a secret," Sofia said quietly, "I mean, I didn't know your dad, but a few people tried to talk to me . . . blah blah blah," she made puppet hands in front of her face. "I just told them to shut up. They were afraid if they asked you, you would sock them like you did Sally."

All of the girls looked at Sally.

"Joy, I know we have already talked about what happened that day when you flattened me, but I REALLY am sorry I said what I said . . . that your dad ran off with someone who wasn't um . . . well, you know. I'm sorry."

"How are you feeling now that you met her?" Ava asked, placing her hand on her friend's arm. "Your stepmom?"

Joy's mouth began to do a nervous twitching. She hadn't thought of her that way. She shrugged her shoulders.

"I think your mom is really nice, and waaaaay prettier!" Sally said. "Who cares that she doesn't have a fancy pants job."

Joy looked at Sally. A hard ball was forming in her throat and her ears were making a crackly sound. She looked over at Sofia, whose dad was a doctor and her mom an accountant. Then, to Ava, whose parents weren't rich, but crazy cool artist types. Only Joy had a mom that was . . . normal . . . and middle class . . . and, since her dad left her after being a homemaker for ten years, the only job she could get . . .

Joy burst into tears. Normally, she would never cry in front of her friends, but it was like every shame she had ever felt just needed to be dug up, roots and all.

"Wait?" Sofia looked confused. "What are you talking about, Sally? Joy's mom works at the office tower?"

Joy took the wrapper from the chocolate crispies and blew her nose into it. All eyes waited to see how Joy would respond.

"Sofia," Joy said quietly, "You know how I never let you come over until it's after dinner, or my mom's at work?"

"Ya," Sofia said, her head tilted, a bit confused.

"It's because I never want you guys to see my mom in her . . . uniform."

"I am confused," Sofia said, her hands lifted up to her shoulders, exasperated.

"Ugh, Sofia, oh my word. What do you think Joy's mom does in the tower?" Ava was more frustrated than compassionate. "Joy's mom cleans all the offices in there!"

"Wow, all by herself?" Sofia said, her eyes huge, "That's mind-blowing! My mom can't even clean our house herself. She has a maid who comes every other Friday."

Sally dropped her head into her hands, "Honestly Sofia, sometimes you're not the sharpest crayon in the box."

"What?" Sofia said, "I think Mrs. Bomb is amazing. I'm serious. So what if she doesn't have a college kind of career. I bet they love her there, and that she doesn't just clean offices, but makes everyone happy when they see her. She makes everyone feel warmer after you talk to her."

Joy looked at her friends.

"Kids are stupid at school," Sally said slowly. "We say things that we hear our parents say sometimes."

"Like, my dad was a gold-digger and ditched my mom for money?" Joy said in an angry tone.

"Yeah," Sally said, nodding.

"You know what, Joy?" Ava began to say as she ripped the head off of one of Sofia's gummy bears, "Adults do stupid things when it comes to love and money and junk."

"Well, what was she like?" Sally asked.

"Oh, we never went in last night. Dad – wow, that feels REALLY weird to say out loud, um, my father came to the fence and talked to us. I realized when he got closer that I had actually bumped into him on Thursday walking to school. But all I saw was his stupid sweater . . ." Joy's voice trailed off. "Anyhow, so yeah, I never realized it was him."

"So, did you hold the baby?" Sofia said with a dreamy smile. "Do they need a babysitter?"

"Joy," Sally looked at her friend, as they all ignored Sofia's comment, "Did your mom tell you that your dad wants to have you sleep over there sometimes? They call it joint custody."

Joy's shoulders slumped down. "Yep. Eventually. When we walked home last night she was waiting for us to finish the talk. I guess the boys knew . . . everyone knew . . . I just never heard anything."

"Maybe because you heard, but your brain didn't want to hear the truth?" Ava said, taking a bite of her chocolate crispie.

"I have something to show you guys," Joy said, reaching into her back pocket, "Here, look at the last two pictures from the mystery thing-a-ma-jig."

The girls all leaned in. "It's HER!" they said in unison.

"Yep."

"But, they look like Robert's age almost?" Ava said, her head leaning in even closer.

Sofia's nose scrunched and her eyes rolled, "Well, duh, that's a college party! Look at the wall behind them."

They all took another look. Sure enough, a college insignia was a bit blurry, but there was no mistaking the mascot.

One mystery was solved, but a bigger question hung in the air.

Chapter 16

Joy stood in front of the bathroom mirror, she had never been so nervous. Not even when she was sitting on the hall floor after flattening Sally, or on her first 'mascara to school day'. Never. This was big.

"What if they think I'm ugly?" Joy said quietly, "What if I make him yell again?" She began to pace. "Oh why did my mom make me give back the mascara?" Joy went back to facing the mirror. She tilted her head every which way like the models do. Under the sink was a basket where Joy kept all her hair pins, elastics and clips. She put it up on the counter and began to part her hair this way and that.

She scrunched it all on top of her hair in a messy bun. When Ava did that, her jet black straight hair looked like an abstract piece of art. When Joy did her poker straight blonde hair, somehow it came out looking like she had slept a few nights on a park bench.

In the rain.

With record breaking winds.

She pulled out the scrunchie and grabbed a few hair clips. Then, recalling the sidewalk episode only days before, she decided to avoid clips around her father.

"Well, this is as good as it gets." She said to no one but herself. She put the basket back under the sink, and went to her room to wait until 01800 hours. Whenever there was a serious thing going down, Sally and Joy had decided to use military time. It seemed fitting to do so tonight.

Joy sat at her desk and flipped the small, butterfly-covered notebook through her fingers, back and forth. The faster she moved it, the butterflies almost seemed to take flight. She took her favorite pencil out of the old, star and moon themed mug that held a variety of pens and pencils. She opened the book to the blank, well-worn first page that had held so many of her secrets.   It looked a bit thin and vulnerable. Kind of like Joy.

She turned to the second page. Pencil lead had never touched this page. It was fresh. New. Full of all kinds of hope. Sharpening her favorite pencil, she began to write.

I have a father.
A real one on the earth.
And he wants to know me.

Joy stared at the words. Her heart began to beat faster. Was it joy she was feeling? Or fear? Maybe both? She began to erase, starting from the last sentence and working backwards. When only the first four words were left, she couldn't bring herself to rub them out. She let the words soak into her bright blue eyes. 'I have a father'.

She took her grey cylinder and tapping the book, watched with satisfaction as the dust tumbled into the dark, mysterious abys of the container.

She sat, holding the book, still taking in the words. Putting down her eraser, she held the book up to her chest, and mouthed the words quietly, "Father God, I have a father, here, on this earth, and . . ." Joy let out a satisfied sigh, "I have his eyes."

"Joy?" the sound of Billy's voice interrupting such an intimate moment with her Heavenly Father, caused Joy to jump. "Are you ready?"

Chapter 17

"Slow down, Joy!" Billy said, "You're gonna dump me off the sidewalk."

Joy had been talking nonstop. "Sorry, well, what do you think? Is it weird that it is only just you and me tonight? Why didn't Steve and Robert come with us?"

"For the kazillionth time, Joy, I don't know, but I think they are still mad at him," Billy said, his arms flailing madly, "I mean it, SLOW DOWN!"

"Wow, for a Bog-boy who wasn't afraid to climb super high in a ridiculously old tall tree . . . by himself . . . you sure have become a scaredy cat."

"Stop it, Joy. I'm kinda nervous. And your crazy driving skills are making me feel worse. Wait. Stop."

Managing to curb her excitement, Joy felt bad for her brother and took her fast trot down to a slow waltz.

"No, I mean it, stop." Billy said, his voice sounded weak.

Joy stopped, locked the brake on his wheelchair, and came to the side to look at his face. "I'm sorry, I was nervous too and I have talked nonstop."

"Your talking isn't the problem," Billy looked like he was going to throw up, "I'm not sure if I want to go tonight anymore."

Joy's eyes grew wide, "What? You can't leave me with two and a half strangers!"

Billy's head dropped, and Joy could see drops falling onto the drone he had brought that was sitting in his lap. "What if they don't want me?"

"What are you even saying?" Joy said, now moving around to the front so she could look him right in the eyes, "You are . . . . BILLY! BILLY! Everyone loves you. You are like, loveable. Even when you make me so mad, I can't ever stay mad at you."

Billy looked up and smiled, wiping a few tears, "Well, that's true, I am pretty amazing. And humble. But, they have a son. I used to be the youngest boy. Now I am just a . . . third born?" He scratched his head.

"Listen, we stick together. That's all we can do. We will never know unless we try."

"You never, never know if you never, never go!" Billy said, nodding, his smile returning with typical confidence.

Joy nodded and moved to the rear of the chair, unlocked it, and began to roll them to some kind of new normal.

Their father was waiting for them at the front picket fence gate.

"Well, there they are!" His voice sounded keen but cautious. He was every bit as nervous as his two kids. "We hope you're hungry and like pizza, because Crystal makes the best homemade pizza ever!"

"We are both lactose intolerant," Billy said with a straight face.

"Oh," Mr. Bomb looked very uneasy. "You would think a father would know that about his own kids."

Joy's tummy began to roll, and her heart burn. She slugged her brother's arm.

"I'm just messing with you," Billy said with a menacing but comical cackle of a laugh, "Gotcha!"

Their father looked mad at first, but then he too broke into a smile. Joy took a deep breath. It was going to be an interesting night.

As their father held open the little gate, Joy was careful to wheel Billy clear of anything that could possibly bump his leg. There was a makeshift ramp up the four stairs leading into the house.

"Here Joy-Bug, that ramp is steep, let me push." As Joy released the responsibility to her father, her two hands went up and held her eyebrows, as if to hold them onto her forehead. She had heard that name before, but not in a very, very long time. As soon as she walked in the house, she quickly asked to use the washroom.

Once locked inside, she pulled out the butterfly book, turning to the second page. Next to the four words that she had bravely left from only minutes before, she added:

I have a father.

and he knows my name

She looked in the mirror at her beautiful blue eyes and smiled. Turning her pencil over to the eraser end, she paused. Looking in the mirror, she smiled even bigger and put the book back in her pocket.

"Well," Jim Bomb said, pushing himself away from the table with a satisfied belly pat. "That was great pizza, wasn't it kids?"

Billy and Joy both looked at their dad, and then at Crystal. The whole dinner was void of any discussion other than, "Danny, no!" and "Danny, don't!" Danny this and Danny that. So busy managing their toddler, the two adults barely even looked at their two young guests.

Unsure as to whether they wanted to give any satisfying validation to the woman who stole their dad away, neither answered.

"Well," Crystal Bomb said nervously, "We have dessert! Who likes strawberry shortcakes?" She grabbed the empty pizza plates and disappeared into the kitchen.

Jim looked very uncomfortable.

"How's it going in there Hon? Do you need any help?"

"No, I've got it. Talk to your kids."

Jim turned to Joy first, "So, Joy-Bug, what grade are you in now?"

"Fifth." Joy snickered. It was an honest answer, but when she said it, it reminded her also of 'pleading the fifth'. They had learned that at school, but Sally really explained it. She was only going to give him answers on a need to know basis until she knew what to expect. After him losing his cool over a sweater, she was being careful.

Clearing his throat, Jim Bomb decided to turn his attention to Billy, "So, when your mom told me you were in surgery, you really gave me quite the scare! I was afraid we might lose you!"

● ● ●

"Yeah?" Billy looked at his dad as he was unhooking the highchair tray, and tussling his blonde boy's curly hair. "So, if you were so scared of losing me, why did you run off to the city seven years ago?"

Joy's body went as stiff as a statue. She couldn't believe Billy just said that. Crystal stood in the doorway, balancing a full tray of scones, strawberries and two containers of compressed whipping cream. Their eyes met. Joy could see terror in Crystal Bomb's eyes.

"Billy," Jim's voice was stern, fatherly.

Crystal walked in between the two, causing a break in their stare down, "Now, that's a fair question for Billy to ask," she said, placing the tray down on the table and making a face at Jim that only he could see.

Jim continued to bounce baby Danny on his lap as his eyes searched the room, making contact with everything except his two older children.

"Well," he said finally, "That is where Crystal grew up, and my business was failing in this town, and . . . we felt it was better for all to create some . . . distance."

Danny began to grab his father's lower lip with stubby, toddler fingers.

"Okay, kids, help yourself. You just build it like this," Crystal wanted to interrupt the awkward discussion. She placed a half of a scone on her plate, scooped some cut up strawberries to cover it, then reached for the whip, "This is the best part!" she made a fancy swoop of cream with the star tip on the compressed container.

She handed her creation to Jim.

"Now you try," she said to the kids. Joy leaned in and put two scones on two plates and made eye contact with Billy as to how many strawberries he wanted. Once he was satisfied, Joy passed the plate to Billy and handed him the whip cream.
PSSSSSTTTTHHH
Billy put a generous amount of the topping on his, raising his curly whipped top with more flare and style than Crystal's.
IT WAS ON. Joy had seen Billy when he was lit and full of wit.
"Well, we may not be as fancy here as in the city, but we know how to do a lot of things better than city folk." He paused, "The only thing the city has that we don't . . . is plenty of . . ." he looked straight at Crystal, "dog parks."
What he said was true. How he said it, and the tone he said it in was not nice.
Crystal's face looked hurt.
Joy's tummy began to tumble, but she also felt a feeling of satisfaction to see the two people who had hurt them so badly, get a taste of pain.
For a brief moment, nobody moved or spoke. Then Crystal, with a calm and grace that the situation did not warrant, took the other whipped container off the table, turned to Billy, and shot him in the face!
Even baby Danny was shocked.
Only the sound of breathing could be heard.
Billy placed his plate on his lap, took his hand across his face, dramatically cleaning just his eyes.
He blinked.

And then, he sprayed his can right back at her. She squealed and shot back. Some of Billy's shots hit his dad's face and Danny's back. Unarmed, the only defense Joy and Jim had was to fling overshot secondhand cream. It didn't even matter who was getting hit, they were all shooting and flinging at whichever target was closest.

And.
Laughing.
Hard!

By the time the canisters ran out of pressure, they all had ran out of steam. Whipping cream was dripping off of everyone and everything.

Tears of glee had cleaned up any cream from their faces though. They all held their tummies from laughing so hard.

"Oh, oh, oh, my stomach!" Billy said, leaning over and groaning in his chair.

"Ohhhhh," Jim said, his voice sounding eerily the same as Billy's. He wiped Danny's hair with a napkin, "I think we all needed that!" Jim looked over at his only daughter and gave her a wink. "What do you think, Joy-Bug?"

"We hit a few snags, but we'll be okay." Joy said, winking back.

Jim groaned, "Oh Joy-Bug, you are too punny!"

Crystal stopped cleaning and looked serious at the newcomers in her home, "You know, its better sometimes to say things in the moment, rather than stuffing it down or saying it behind people's backs. I know our choices hurt you kids, and I am so sorry. But it is good that Billy was honest about his feelings." She gave him a swat with the tea towel, "But if you ever get cheeky with me again, it will be more than just whipping cream you'll have to watch out for!"

Billy laughed and his face gave her a sincere smile, "I am impressed. I deserved what I got. I should have got worse."

Jim's voice and face got serious, "I know not everything can be fixed with a good food fight, but do you think over time you kids will someday forgive me for running away?"

Billy looked at his sister, a weak smile appeared on her face, and she motioned to him to speak for them both.

"Yeah, maybe. We have a lot of questions, but we can work on it. Hey, since you owe us a bunch of Christmas gifts, how about you buy us a dog?" Billy looked at Crystal and let out his unique cackle of a laugh.

Smiling now, Crystal tossed the tea towel with amazing skill, covering Billy's head.

Jim laughed, it sounded just like Billy's chortle.

Joy sat back, taking in the people around the table. It wasn't a perfect picture, but somehow, they were becoming a family. They had all made mistakes that had caused pain, but yet something – or someone – brought them all back together. They had all found something tonight.

Something none of them knew was missing, except maybe Billy. His soul knew what he needed – his dad.

Joy reached into her back pocket and took out her book and pencil.

● ● ●

I have a father.

and he knows my name

and he loves me

Hello God? Can I tell You something...

I know things are still going to be bumpy. Tonight went okay. I still don't like Crystal, but I don't hate her anymore. It was weird to know dad loved someone before he met mom.

I guess even adults get scared when they fail at things and make mistakes. Is it bad that I felt good over there? Does that mean I am not loyal to mom?

> **Books I am reading or Bible Verses**
> John 17:11
> Romans 8:28
> John 3:16

Billy's leg is mending, and I think our family is too. It just may not look the way it used to, but we will figure it out.

Oh, and Danny. He's so super cute. And, HE LOOKS LIKE ME! Blonde and blue eyes!

Today I feel

Gratitude and Thanks

*That You are fixing broken things

*That my heart feels full whenever I hear, JOY-BUG

You allow people to make choices that can sometimes hurt themselves, or others. Like Billy climbing a tree, or me using expired makeup, ditching my friends . . . or even Dad running away from us and his problems.

What is God saying to me about this?

None of us are perfect? Gosh. No kidding. Sorry, Father, I mean, yes. You are right.

You love us, and loving parents let their kids say what's on their hearts, even if it sometimes ends up in a mess before it gets better. And, when we do make bad choices, You manage to bring us back to a place where we can choose to ask forgiveness from You and others. Which is okay . . . even though rolling the world backwards may be something You may want to try sometime.

Wait? What?! Once You DID turn the world and time backwards? I guess we have our next topic for Mrs. S!

Since You're listening, I kinda need . . .

*You to help my mom get Jesus out of the penalty box!

Thank You for hearing & loving me!

How did you like Joy's story?

She certainly can get confused, just like we all can! But God *IS* good, isn't He? Religion can be confusing too, which is why I hope this book helped you find *friendship* with God. Relationship is what God is all about. He made and LOVES humans!

Sitting with God every day, it should never get boring or stale. If you didn't really enjoy your time with Him, is it possible that you were doing too much talking and not enough listening?

Imagine if when we went to school, we sat in front of our teacher and blabbered on all day, never letting him speak. How much would we learn? At the end of the year, would we have matured and grown in any way? Maybe some, but I would think the teacher would be fired pretty quickly if nobody listened to him . . . If you didn't already know, there is a book called the Bible. God placed a lot of important stuff in there and He speaks to us through it. Since God wrote it, people call it His Word. I think of it as God's love letter to me. He explains that He is three Persons in One; Father, Son (Jesus) and Holy Spirit. That may be confusing, but if it helps, think about an egg. There is a yolk, egg white and the shell, yet altogether, they make one egg. And they function as one and need each other!

That may be lame, but hopefully it helps.

So, this God that you have been writing to, and hopefully listening to, He not only gave us a book that explains a lot about Himself, ourselves and our world, but God the Father also sent His Son, Jesus, to come to the earth and save us, (draw us close to Him).

The Bible says that all have sinned and come short of the glory of God. That is a fancy way of saying that there is no one that is perfect. (Not even your sometimes "perfect" sibling that everyone wishes you were more like). No. No one means no one. This is a deep thing, but let's face it, we've all done wrong things. Before we even entered preschool we probably stole a cookie!

And God is holy. That means HE IS PERFECT, and He so wants us to not just sit on a lovely, soft, blue velvet chair, but He longs for us to jump up into His lap! But first, we need to deal with our sin – because He couldn't take us up into his lap covered in "dirt".

So Jesus, He came, lived and walked on the earth, just like we do. He felt hungry, tired, and I even think He may have stubbed his toe more than once since they walked in sandals back then. Yet, Jesus did not sin. The Bible said He lived a perfect life.

Now, this is where it gets a bit gross and sad. Jesus had to die for our sins . . . the Bible says the blood He spilled washes away our sin. Trust me. It doesn't make sense, but it is true.

But guess what? He didn't stay dead! Holy Spirit – the third part of God, rose Him up back to life. We've all heard of people getting their heart restarted by paramedics, well, this wasn't that. Jesus was dead for 3 whole days. This was a miracle from God . . . and was ALWAYS God's plan. Father sent Him. Jesus laid down His life and died for us. Holy Spirit breathed life back into Jesus! The Three-In-One God working together perfectly.

Anyhow, this is a pretty quick recap of what being a "Christian" is. We believe that Jesus came, died, and rose again, and we ask Him to be Lord (boss) of our lives. I actually don't say I am a Christian – I like to say I am a Jesus follower. I want my life to look like His, not just look like a religious person!

Here is a simple prayer if you aren't sure whether or not you've made Jesus Your Savior and Lord:

Hello God,

I know I am not perfect. I need Jesus to wash me and make me clean so I can come close to You!

I believe that Jesus came to earth (we celebrate His birth at Christmas!) and that He lived a perfect life. Then, because He was so good, He laid down his life and died, but YAY – Holy Spirit breathed life into Him and He rose again (we celebrate His rising back to life at Easter!)

I need You God – Father, Jesus and Holy Spirit. Please be a part of my life every day. Keep teaching and speaking to me. Help me to read and understand Your Bible and to tell others how good it is to know You. Like, REALLY know You.

Thanks for being my best friend and for always listening. I ask You these things in Jesus' name. (Sorry to be such a name dropper, but Jesus told us to use His name as it gets us out of a lot of trouble, and into a lot of great places – like heaven!) Amen (that means – let it be so!)

PS: I love You too!

If you've prayed this prayer,
Please email JoyBomb@pm.me

God Loves YOU!

WATCH FOR MORE of JOY BOMB'S OWN JOURNAL BOOKS COMING SOON ON AMAZON!

(CAN YOU EVEN BELIEVE SHE WOULD SHARE THESE?)

Mrs. Solomon's Wise Words

(There is a lot here! Don't try to answer them all at once or your brains may fall out!)

1. Assumptions and rumors can make messes. Can you recall some from the story? Have you ever made mistakes or listened or spread rumors?

2. Joy believed God had given her a tube of mascara. Did He? Go back and read the Journal on pages 66 & 67.

3. Emotions are important. Sometimes they make us feel uncomfortable and we may want to ignore them, but we shouldn't. Even good emotions need to be addressed and not denied. (Like when we may have a crush on someone). Talk about that with someone.

4. Joy's besties saw Joy for who she was, and didn't care what she wore or whether or not she had a "flat-face". ☺ Her new friends came with a set of rules for how Joy was to behave and with expectations to change in order to be accepted. Have you ever experienced that?

5. Joy was mad at her dad for ditching her as a kid, but then Joy ditched her friends too. Did you notice that? Sometimes we all can make bad choices.

6. Joy wanted to throw a stone at her dad's window. Do you know there is a Bible verse about that? Did you read John 8:7 from Joy's journal? What do you think Holy Spirit was saying to Joy that night?

7. When Joy was sad, her friends didn't try to fix it or make Joy feel better. They sat quietly with her and joined her in her pain. Why was that a good thing?

8. Things break; legs, families, hearts, churches and friendships. The important thing to remember is that most of the time, things can be mended, and over time, many can heal. Joy and Billy went to see their dad, but the older boys needed more time to process. What do you think about that?

9. Joy was upset when her mom said bad things about herself and called herself a 'hag'. Yet, Joy often says mean things to herself! Why do you think we can speak so unkindly to ourselves?

10. Joy thought her mom won the lottery and that they might move into a mansion. Do you think Joy is content in her life, or do you think she wants more fancy things?

11. Joy complained a lot to God about her Grandmother's cooking, but then decided she should maybe put on an apron and become part of the solution. Did you catch that? Do you think God should just fix everything for us or do you think He hopes we will get involved and be His hands and feet sometimes?

12. What do you think the girls did for their secret hand signal to meet up on the roof? Can you guess or make one up with your friends?

13. Not having a parent in your house or in your life can be hard. Joy knows that. You will find as you follow Joy in her journey that just because Jim Bomb moved back, things aren't perfect yet in her life. That is why knowing her Heavenly Father is so important to Joy, and can be for you too! He is always listening. He is never too busy to make time for you. Keep talking and listening to God! He really DOES love you!

Manufactured by Amazon.ca
Bolton, ON